Plays by Lars Norén

Blood

War

**Other Chaucer Press Books by Lars Norén
Translated from Swedish to English by
Marita Lindholm Gochman**

Two Plays: And Give Us the Shadows and
Autumn and Winter (Spring 2013)

Three Plays: Demons, Act, and Terminal 3 (Spring 2014)

Plays by Lars Norén

Blood

War

Translated by

Marita Lindholm Gochman

Chaucer Press Books

An Imprint of Richard Altschuler & Associates, Inc.

Los Angeles

Plays by Lars Norén: Blood and War. Copyright © 2014 by Marita Lindholm Gochman. For information and special orders contact the publisher, Richard Altschuler & Associates, Inc., at richard.altschuler@gmail.com, 10390 Wilshire Boulevard, Suite 414, Los Angeles, CA 90024, or 424-279-9118.

The translation cost for this book was defrayed by a grant from the Swedish Arts Council, gratefully acknowledged.

ISBN-13: 978-1-884092-89-3

Library of Congress Control Number: 2014946989

CIP data for this book are available from the Library of Congress

Chaucer Press Books is an imprint of Richard Altschuler & Associates, Inc.

Cover Design: Josh Garfield

Printed in the United States of America

Dedication

In memory of my beloved parents for having instilled in me an abhorrence toward violence, oppression and war through their brave personal actions during World War 2.

Thank you, Lars, for reminding the world to be mindful of its horrors.

Contents

Foreword

by

David Van Asselt

In 2006, I had the opportunity to visit Sweden. I stayed in a small hotel along the waterfront facing the old city. I had come to meet Lars Norén and watch some of his rehearsals. He was directing *Little Eyolf* at the time for the Riks Drama, a production that would tour Sweden during 2006-07. The morning I was to meet him, I was called down to the front desk because a fax was waiting for me, a hand written note from Lars, telling me how to get to the rehearsal space and how the day would go. Up to that moment I had been just another anonymous American tourist, but that morning the entire staff of the hotel had assembled to see just who this person was, to receive a note from Sweden's leading play- wright. Though I had known and read Lars' work prior to coming, I shall never forget the looks on those faces and the respect they showed me from that moment forward. It brought home, in a way perhaps nothing else could, just how great an artist Lars Norén was and continues to be, not only in Sweden but throughout Europe. He is, simply, the greatest Swedish dramatist since August Strindberg. It remains a mystery why he is not better known in the U.S.

Lars Norén was born in Stockholm in 1944 and began by writing poetry and novels, but when he made the final move into drama after 1980, he found the medium where his true genius lay. Beginning with *The Courage to Kill*, continuing with his first success *Night is the Mother to the Day*, Norén created a series of plays detailing the love-hate relationships within families, characters imprisoned within self-contained hells, in a style that fused elements of Eugene O'Neill with Edward Albee but was, of course uniquely Norén. By the time of *Blood* and *Romanians* (both 1994), he had begun to move out of the claustrophobic family residence and into the wider world.

Written in response to the disappearances and torture in South America, *Blood* can be seen as a kind of family drama with a difference. Here Norén uses the family to get at larger issues, to examine the effect of torture and violence on a couple who have lost their son and seem forever condemned to play out their past without being able to break free of a crime. Contrary to a classical dramatic figure, such as Oedipus, who was the victim of fate, there is nothing necessary in the fates of these contemporary citizens, singled out and doomed to exile.

With the 1997 six hour epic *Personae 3:1*, he created a whole world populated by outsiders, prostitutes, drug addicts, and prisoners, giving a voice to Sweden's outcasts and immigrants. Then in *7:3* he used actual prisoners on government-arranged furloughs to create a play, though the experiment ended with tragically unintended results. On the day after the final performance, two of the three felons robbed a bank. A guard was killed, triggering a national debate. Norén's response was to delve more deeply into this world, writing another play set in a prison, and *Cold*, a play detailing how three neo-Nazi youths goad themselves into beating a Korean immigrant.

In 2003, in response to the Bosnian genocide, he wrote *War*. In common with *Blood*, it examines the way war tears a family apart, creating scars that can never be healed. *War* is remarkable for the simplicity with which it is able to paint a portrait of the horrors inflicted on one family. By telling his story without sentimentality and through language that is spare and matter of fact, the pain of this family is brought home in a way that is truthful but has the weight of a Greek tragedy. Taking place over a few days, we are witnesses to how one family survives through the small amount of time presented on stage. Small events happen. A father, thought to be dead, returns, blinded after having been forced into a work camp. His wife has already moved on. Their children hover between their desire for a lost childhood and the brutality of their new existence. It's a devastating portrait. With only a few slight changes in place names, this play could be set in Iraq, in Guatemala, in Libya, in Cambodia, in literally a thousand places throughout the globe. Its truth would remain the same.

We produced *War* at Rattlestick Playwrights Theater in New York in 2009. Originally my journey to Sweden was to enlist Lars to come to the U.S. and direct a play. *War* was the one we settled on. His idea was to direct it in a way that was much more cruel than the written text. And watching the rapport he had with his actors, the absolute trust they had in him, and the emotional places they were willing to explore still makes me wonder what we might have achieved had he been able to come. Unfortunately illness interceded and by that time we were too far along to cancel. As it was, we had the invaluable help of Lars' longtime collaborator Ulrika Josephsson, a terrific director in her own right. And we had the wonderful Marita Lindholm Gochman in the room with us, always able to explain a phrase and find ways to make her translation both more accurate and easier to perform. The production remains one which I will treasure for the rest of my life.

David Van Asselt
Artistic Director
Rattlestick Playwrights Theater
New York City

Translator's Introduction

by

Marita Lindholm Gochman

Blood and war, war and blood—two words that seem connected in a most terrifying way. The two plays *Blood* and *War* by Lars Norén are both terrifying in their descriptions of what happens during political uprisings and unrest.

Blood was written in the early nineties, when the war in the Balkans was raging and the AIDS epidemic seemed to be at its peak. *War* had its world premiere at the *Théâtre des Amandiers* in Nanterre, France, in 2003, when most of the world was engaged in the issues concerning the Middle East and what would ultimately lead to the controversial American invasion of Iraq.

Both plays have their roots in political discontent, but Norén's outrage is mostly manifested in his anti-war, anti-violence stand, and is not necessarily meant to be an analysis of political maneuvers by governments. He is interested in personal issues during periods of extraordinary and violent circumstances, which will forever change the lives of the characters.

I remember an extremely cold week in January 1996 in Malmo, Sweden. My husband and I had traveled there to attend the premiere of *Blood* at Malmo City Theater. Lars had also come down from Stockholm to see the play in its first production. I had brought an early draft of my translation to discuss with Lars, and I was very interested in finding out how the Malmo City Theater would approach this complicated play. The cold weather outside seemed to correspond to the chilly production inside the theater. As far as I remember, the evening seemed bloodless, strangely enough—the absolute opposite of what I had imagined while working on the translation back in the US.

Blood is the story of a Chilean couple, sympathizers of Allende, who had been imprisoned after the coup by Pinochet in 1973, lost contact with their young son at that time, and later moved to Paris. We meet the couple after they had been living in Paris for twenty years, when the woman, a famous war journalist, has just published a book about her experiences in Chile. The play opens and closes with TV interviews taking place—comments on the sensationalism that prevails in TV newscasts.

I don't remember discussing the Malmo production with Lars, but I know that we talked about the upcoming workshop of *Blood* in New York, in the summer of 1996, which was going to be directed by the Swedish director Bjorn Melander. The workshop was hosted by the Circle in the Square Theater and its artistic director, Ted Mann; and we had a cast of wonderful Hispanic-American actors in the leading roles. Bjorn Melander had directed many important Norén productions in Sweden, and his long experience really helped the actors get a grasp of how to approach the Norén characters in a short amount of time. The New York workshop production turned out to be the opposite of the Swedish production—very hot, blood boiling, and quite controversial.

Bjorn Melander's assistant director was a young Juilliard graduate, Ben Krevolin, who later wrote an interesting article for *The Juilliard Journal*, in October 1996, about *Blood* and his experience working with Bjorn. Here is a short excerpt from his article: "*Blood* exists in a complex emotional landscape where the elusive search for love and the power of past events inescapably lead to brutal force. Or does it? The play challenges the audience on political, sexual, psychological, historical and mythical levels."

What really struck me about *Blood* this time around were the ingenious ways Lars had made use of the title—blood in the family ties, HIV-infected blood, hospital blood, blood spilled in violence and war, and, finally, the lust for blood by the public shown on television and in the tabloids. Greek drama obviously represents the basic framework for this play, as Lars has always found inspiration in the Greek myths, beginning with his earliest plays.

The Rattlestick Playwright's Theater in New York had expressed interest in producing a Norén play. The artistic director, David van Asselt, decided that *War* was the play he wanted to produce. When I got the message from David, I called Lars in Stockholm and he said that he was interested in directing the New York production. I can't describe how happy it made me to hear Lars say that. Finally, Lars would be able to spend time in New York, and we would have a chance to introduce this elusive playwright to the American public. Well, that did not happen. Lars, unfortunately, fell ill and we had to scramble to find a director willing to take his place.

By the time the rehearsals began in January 2009, the war in Iraq was winding down. It seemed like the timing for this play would be perfect and its impact might be of importance, but the reception in New York was muted. Maybe the idea of this ordinary family living through the hell of war didn't connect with an American audience. In Europe the play had left the audiences both shaken and amused. To them the play seemed to bring the horror as well as the craziness and lunacy of war into focus. According to my friend Ulrika Josephsson, Lars Norén's longtime producer in Sweden, many of the emigrants from former Yugoslavia who saw the Swedish production came up to her and told her how much the story was like their own. They asked her how Lars Norén could possibly have known about their lives and their problems.

After having worked with Lars for thirty years, I can attest to the fact that "LARS KNOWS!" I don't know how, but he seems to be absorbing, with all his being, not only the human horror stories in our Western world, but also most everything that's going on in politics, art, music, fashion, and even pop culture.

I think that *War*, in its simplicity and honesty, brings the message home about the absolute craziness and foolishness of war—and also, in the midst of hell, a tiny ray of hope sprouting in the form of impossible love.

As far as the translation process for *Blood* and *War*, I had followed my usual pattern, with a first draft, a "read through" with my husband, a table read through with actors, a second draft, and a workshop.

When I now reread my translation of *Blood*, I am surprised by how formal and foreign it seems. Did twenty years change me, or had those years changed the language, or had the meaning of certain words shifted or changed their colors? Rereading *War* feels different. The work on that translation was more recent, and we had continued to sharpen the text during the whole rehearsal process at the Rattlestick Playwright's Theater. Many of the solutions to simple, everyday language really come from working with directors and actors. The better the actors get to know their characters the better they become at finding the right language. However, this was not true for *Blood*. In this play the actors needed to accept the language given to them. The language is just the "tip of the iceberg," as the Swedish director Bjorn Melander always says when working on Norén plays. In this play, *Blood*, filled with unfinished sentences and unspoken thoughts—and yet populated by extremely verbal characters—the language has to be clear and precise.

In my quest to bring awareness of Lars Norén's remarkable body of work to an American audience, I have been reading up on what recently has been said about him by Swedish theater critics and theater professionals. An excellent newly published source on Norén is the two-volume collection of his plays called *Samhalle* (Community or Society) and *Terminal* (Terminal), which contain valuable commentary in the afterwords (Albert Bonniers Forlag, 2014). In *Samhalle*, the Swedish film director Kristian Petri says the following about Norén's plays: "Very often I meet characters in these texts who are stuck in some 'dead end' alley way, stuck in something beyond their control. Many Norén plays begin with the characters waking up seemingly from a nightmare, or rather—waking up inside a nightmare." In *Terminal*, the Swedish critic and journalist Mikael von Reis says, regarding Norén's extraordinary body of work, that we can now begin to look back on more than one hundred plays—about marriages coming apart, siblings, mothers and fathers, family gatherings, middle class people branching out into or disappearing from society, with their condemnations and disappointments—and see that Norén leaves and returns to ground he has just stepped on. We feel and hear the rhythms and the music in his investigations of human beings with all their inconsistencies in place. "I live in leave-taking . . . my work is leave-taking," Norén has said about his plays. "To write is to both return and to leave."

It seems to me that you have to enter the Norén universe—which is easy to resist because you have to go to such dark and painful places within yourself (with your sense of humor intact)—to become aware of the inconsistency and contradiction in human existence. Lars doesn't explain, he exposes, he holds up a mirror for us to glance at our often dangerously silly and peculiar behavior. He makes us aware of how fragile our life on earth is, how thin the line is between some kind of normalcy and hell. He seems to understand the fleeting nature of our lives, little missteps, break-ups, accidents, natural disasters, being in the wrong place at the wrong time, being an outsider, addictions, criminality and mental instability—all themes he explores in his writing.

BLOOD

Characters

Rosa, a journalist

Eric, a psychiatrist

Madeleine H, a TV interviewer

Luca, a medical student

The Voice of Claude, a patient of Eric

The Voice of Emile, a patient of Eric

A TV Crew

1.

Rosa is seated in a chair in a brightly lit TV studio; across from her is the interviewer, Madeleine H. They are both about the same age. Rosa's hair is short and dark. She is beautiful and very fit, perhaps even a little too thin. She is dressed in a dark blue suit. She seems relaxed, almost indifferent. Soon she'll be choosing her words with great care and ease. At this point we don't really hear what they are talking about. Mostly they are exchanging niceties; they smile at each other—perhaps they are talking about the upcoming summer, places to go on vacation, fashion, the weather. The interviewer offers Rosa a glass of bottled water. Rosa asks if it has gas in it and says she doesn't want mineral water with gas.

ROSA
Why bubbles? They aren't necessary. (*We get a feeling that there are a number of people working around them in the studio. On the table sits the book that Rosa has written, which is the reason for the interview.*)

(At the same time, Eric is entering the living room after having changed clothes in the bedroom. He is dressed in grey jeans, a black T-shirt and a dark-blue cashmere sweater, and is sniffing a new deodorant he just bought that he has taken out of a plastic bag. Unscrewing the cap, he makes a grimace, as he finds the scent much too sweet, but he none- theless dabs a little on his wrist. From the same plastic bag he also takes out a couple of books, three CDs—"The Goldberg Variations," "The Four Seasons," and the film music from "The Blue Film." He then walks over and pours himself a glass of wine, disappears, comes back, and opens a window, but no sounds from the outside are heard. He uses the remote control to start the CD of Maurizio Pollini playing "Schubert's Sonata in D Sharp," as he passes by. He is barefoot. He stops, takes a sip of the wine, then puts the glass down. He goes and fetches another plastic bag from which he takes out a jacket he has just bought, and is thinking of trying it on, but doesn't. Instead, he hangs it on a chair, looks at it, then forgets about it. He walks over to the book shelves, picks out Cioran's History and Utopia, *and looks for a sentence he had previously underlined. Then he takes out* Self Examinations *by Marcus Aurelius and then* The Jewish Mystique *by Scholem Alechem. He puts all three books on the big dining room table, is looking calm, almost happy, and remains*

*where he is. There is a slight sense of uneasiness emanating from his be-
ing, as if he was trying in vain to remember a sentence he once knew. He
uses the remote control, which he has been holding through the whole
scene, to activate the playback on the telephone answering machine, and
at the same time he turns on the TV and notices the program title
"Imago." Then he hears his own voice, and is looking at Rosa's calm
face while listening to his own voice, which is calm, serious and thought-
ful. Slowly he lowers the sound of Schubert.)*

ERIC'S VOICE
(*on a telephone answering machine*) This is Eric Sabato. I can't come to
the phone right now, but please leave your name and phone number and
I'll call you right back. Please wait for the beep. Thank you.

MADELEINE H
(*She smiles quickly at Rosa, then turns toward the camera, which now
shows the red "on" light, and looks into it calmly, as if it were a trusted
colleague.*) Good evening. . . . Welcome to Imago. Tonight we are happy
to welcome a fascinating guest making a rare TV appearance . . . a
woman who, in spite of the fact that she's known more for asking questions than answering them, has graciously agreed to join us here tonight.
She's the journalist and author, Rosa Sabato. (*She turns to Rosa, who's
now on camera.*) Welcome to Imago.

ROSA
Thank you.

MADELEINE H
Yes, we're very pleased and happy that you're here to talk about your
new book. . . . Well, let me first say that you have, for many years, been
celebrated, even internationally, for your reporting of major stories from
different war zones . . . Beirut, Afghanistan, Guatemala, Angola . . . and
now, just this last winter, your TV programs from war-torn Sarajevo. . . .
Later in the program I'd like to return to the special difficulties you must
run into, not only as a journalist, but a woman journalist, in the hell holes
of the world. . . . But it's not in your role as a leading French journalist,
and one of the bravest, that you're here tonight, but because you have
recently published a . . . shall we call it a novel or maybe rather an

autobiographical tale . . . that has received remarkable attention and has been hailed as a splendidly naked and revealing book about a woman's life and fate under a military dictatorship.

CLAUDE'S VOICE

(*on a telephone answering machine, speaking slowly, sounding very hoarse*) Hello . . . it's Claude. I don't think I'll be able to make it tomorrow. I've got a terrible case of the flu. . . . I don't think I'll ever be well again . . . but if I live, I'll see you next week.

MADELEINE H

Your last book was based on your reports from the war in Guatemala, but this is your first novel. . . . Why did you choose the format of a novel to tell about events that, as far as I can understand, are based on facts and realities? Was it, perhaps, that you could more easily achieve a distance to your own fate, or . . .

ROSA

Yes . . . I had reached a critical moment in my life, when I felt . . . well, some kind of emptiness . . . where I felt . . . where I admitted to myself a growing need to stop for a while and look at events and experiences that had shaped the person I am today . . . both as a private individual and as a professional . . . to search in the chaos for the substance that binds together the significant memories that ultimately forms a life. . . . If you've lived this long under stress and extreme tension, and you've made every effort to try to understand and relate to the human and social catastrophes, as I have—you really are 'on call' constantly, like in an ER, just trying to do what's minimally essential—you realize, with great dismay, that you've neglected yourself; you don't really exist any longer as a human being, since you haven't had the time to understand how what is happening is affecting you . . . and you feel like you've lost yourself. . . . After all, isn't who you are, what should guide you? . . . As a journalist you easily turn into a machine, someone who can't hang on to emotions for too long, because if you do you wouldn't be able to go on. . . . But, on the other hand, in order to try to depict and understand the suffering, the often meaningless suffering, without feeling anything, that's not possible either. I could've tried to find some anesthetic or I could've become emotionally burnt out . . . cynical—it's very easy to

stop feeling when you can't affect any changes—or I could actively
search for the reasons my life turned out this way . . . how I, personally,
have been affected by my experiences . . . like waves creating patterns at
the bottom of the sea. . . . I mean (*laughs*) to be "burned out" is really a
terrible state of mind, something I would do anything to avoid. You have
to, as long as you possibly can, view every new inferno with fresh eyes,
in order to honestly report its horrors.

MADELEINE H
Your book has been described as an intense novel about the fate of one
woman during a time of ruthless transformation, and its central theme is
very much about your own painful experiences in Chile during the sev-
enties. . . . You begin by describing your childhood and adolescence in
Santiago de Chile during the fifties and sixties, where you grew up in a
rather liberal, well-to-do, middleclass household with European values.

ROSA
(*smiles*) Yes, whatever they are. European classical literature and music,
piano lessons . . . respect for education and a general, liberal attitude.

MADELEINE H
Yes. I guess one could say that you had a rather harmonious childhood.

ROSA
Yes, very harmonious. . . . My father was an engineer, my mother a
physician. . . . My childhood was very happy and protected. I was an
only child. I almost never met people who had less than we did. I don't
think I even knew they existed.

MADELEINE H
Your father was a professor at the Academy of Engineering. . . . And
during the sixties you were studying political science at the university. I
gather it was there that you eventually both met your husband and
became interested in the current socialistic ideas and criticisms of society, ideas that didn't only manifest themselves in Europe—well,
mainly in Paris. Here in Paris we remember when ten million workers
demonstrated in the streets and factories, but that also took hold in Central and South America.

ROSA

I guess the demonstrations were even more violent in South America, with Castro, Che Guevara . . .

MADELEINE H

Yeah . . . Che Guevara was a big name during the sixties, almost a kind of saint. . . . But then you started to work more actively for Allende's People's Front—Salvador Allende, who later became the first democratically elected President of Chile.

EMILE'S VOICE

(*on a telephone answering machine*) This is Emile. (*pause*) Sorry to call when I know you aren't at home. Right now I'm supposed to be on the couch at *Rue Bonaparte*. But I'm at home. I've swallowed forty Oxycodones and I'll soon be asleep. (*pause*) How do you say good-bye? (*laughs*) How do you say farewell to someone who's done everything in his power to try to delay the moment when the one who can't take it anymore chooses to give up? . . . Really, I promise you, without despair. . . . I'm just feeling indifferent. I'm trying not to throw up. I want to look nice and clean when they find me. (*pause*) I know that you've been worried, even though you've tried to hide it. You've helped me enough. Now you have to leave me alone! (*pause*) I would've been dead long ago if not for you. (*pause*) Eric . . . Eric . . . this is the first time I'm saying your name. . . . Good bye. . . . Farewell. (*laughs again*) I'm so sorry I've squandered your time . . . and mine. (*short pause*) Thank you.

ROSA

I was nineteen, I think, when I started to work with Allende's Democratic Alliance. At that time all the young people you met were politically engaged. All you talked about was politics. You didn't ask what movie or what kind of music they liked, but what socialistic faction they belonged to, and then you knew who they were. . . . I belonged to a group that organized education for the very poor, the ones who lived in the streets and on garbage heaps; tried to teach them to read and clean house. . . . We were all students, and we honestly believed then that it was possible to change our society in a democratic, socialistic direction.

MADELEINE H
So, you really were a convinced socialist . . . How then do you view . . .

ROSA
Well, a socialist . . . very much to the left anyway. That's how it was
then. There were no other instruments. If you were young and open
minded it was easy to be infected by socialism, but our beliefs were
different from the reality we know today. And we don't know how it
might have developed in Chile . . . had not everyone who embodied a
longing for freedom and justice been murdered, removed or, like me,
forced to go into exile.

(*Eric has walked over to the telephone. He dials the same number over
and over again, but the line is busy.*)

MADELEINE H
Do you think it could have ended up like in Cuba or Nicaragua?

(*Eric puts down the receiver.*)

ROSA
Maybe, it's very likely. (*without changing her tone of voice*) I was
probably a very meek Marxist, without any deep, ideological knowledge.
. . . I guess it was the daily exposure to how people went under due to
poverty and destitution, how our society was built on the fact that a big
part of the population was being exploited that made me want to be
engaged. . . . Every day on the bus on my way to the university from
where my family lived I saw a hellhole of hunger, illness and despair. . . .
It's strange how suddenly one day you understand something that you've
seen all your life, yet never noticed before. . . . At the university there
were only people from my own socioeconomic class that had access to
an education. We read . . . we read Fanon, Lacouture, Althusser, Lukacs,
Mao . . . I don't remember them all.

ROSA'S VOICE
(*At the same time, she is heard on a telephone answering machine.*)
Don't forget me tonight, nine PM, Channel 23. I'd feel much more

secure if I knew your eyes were looking at me. . . . Now I'm sorry I said
yes. . . . I'll hurry back home, love you.

MADELEINE H

However, in spite of the enthusiasm of the people who backed him, I
guess that Allende failed to solve the basic financial problems; but in
order to save the country from ending up in the same political chaos as
many of its neighbors, he ultimately did get the support from a majority
of the Chilean people? Well, let's not dwell on that . . . but the political
climate hardened considerably, and many of Allende's supporters were
arrested and imprisoned.

ROSA

Yes.

MADELEINE H

And you were one of them. Together with your husband, you were
arrested right after the "coup."

ROSA

Yes, I was one of the thousands of people who were taken to *Estadio
Nacional*.

MADELEINE H

One of the photographs from there is now famous.

ROSA

I've looked for my face in those photos, but I've never found it, though I
was there. We were there for fifty-six days. We were abused, we were
cold and hungry, and the guards treated us as if we were cattle. Then I
was taken to the Dawson Station, and I was incarcerated for seventeen
months, my husband and I, and thousands of other people . . . were
interrogated and tortured. (*smiles*) So, if in no other way than being
tortured, I finally became a member of the oppressed class. When it con-
cerned my husband and myself, they were particularly careful to punish
us severely, since we are also Jews.

LUCA'S VOICE

(*on a telephone answering machine*) Hello, it's me. Did you forget me? I was almost sure you'd come over yesterday, that's why I skipped class. But you didn't. It really is difficult for me to organize my day, when I have to spend it waiting for someone who doesn't show up. Just wanted to tell you I had the test done today, for your sake. I'll know in ten days, if you're worried, but I don't think you are. You're so old . . . anyway, you're so old, you'll soon die. (*laughs*) I felt like I did a pregnancy test. . . . I love you (*pause*) even though you're an old fart.

MADELEINE H

(*picks up the book*) I would like to return to your book. The title is *Shadow of Our Time*.

ROSA

Yes . . . I think you can say that many of us who live in exile, and who have carved out lives in other countries, do not experience ourselves as much more than shadows. We live lives in some kind of shadow, which we can't really explain to the people we meet in our new homeland; they just wouldn't understand. . . . We're shadows both in the new country . . . and leftover shadows in the old country, where we weren't allowed to live. (*a little laugh*) I'm a "French speaking shadow." I'm very grateful that my parents gave me a solid education so that I managed emigration relatively well. After all, on the surface it seemed like a short move within the same cultural sphere . . . but you can't bring with you the real essence. And the way the world looks today it only seems to generate more and more refugees. (*laughs a little*) A couple of years ago I happened to be leafing through a history book from the Stalin era, and there was a photograph from some communist celebration during the thirties, when all the top Kremlin leaders were gathered—Stalin in the middle—there to view a military parade. There was something strange about that picture. At first I didn't see it, but in the empty spaces you could clearly see people's shadows on the wall; one even wore an officer's hat. Of course, those were shadows of members of the top communists who had been retouched out of the picture, after they had fallen out of favor. . . . That's how it is with us too, we who fled or who were murdered; we are obliterated, but here and there one can still see our shadows.

LUCA'S VOICE

(on a telephone answering machine) Sorry. Sorry I sounded so bitter. It's just that I feel so alone and afraid. I hate feeling abandoned. *(pause)* I'm always looking for an epilogue. *(pause)* I love you and I'm waiting for you. I'm still young, I've got plenty of time. I'll be waiting for you until you tell me to stop.

MADELEINE H

The book is . . . now we're closing in on a very difficult and sensitive chapter . . . the one devoted to your son, who disappeared in 1974. . . .

(Eric turns up the TV sound.)

(Madeleine H continues.) Your son, who you and your husband had to leave behind in Chile, when the two of you suddenly were expelled . . . ah . . .

ROSA

In October 1974, we arrived in Paris in October 1974.

MADELEINE H

That's right, October 1974, when you were expelled and came to France.

ROSA

But we'd already lost touch with him when we were arrested.

MADELEINE H

How old was he then?

ROSA

He'd just had his eighth birthday.

MADELEINE H

So there was no possibility for you to bring him with you?

ROSA

No. *(pause)* We weren't allowed. *(short pause)* He was taken from us when we were arrested.

MADELEINE H

And since then, since 1973, you've never seen him?

ROSA

No.

MADELEINE H

You don't know anything about his fate . . . what might have happened
to him?

ROSA

No. Nothing.

MADELEINE H

Not where he lives or how he's doing . . . or if he's even alive?

ROSA

No. Nothing. Absolutely nothing. I don't know anything. He was in the
hospital when we were arrested. My parents went there to visit him, but
they weren't even allowed in . . . since we . . . we didn't exist.

MADELEINE H

What do you think might have happened to him?

ROSA

I don't know. . . . The last time I saw him was at the end of August,
1973. That's twenty years ago. . . . So, now he's all grown up. (*pause*)
Some years ago, when Chile once again became somewhat civilized and
the fascists were forgiven . . . even celebrated—when their deed, so to
speak, was completed—it always seems to be a matter of time; they
threw amnesty at us. My husband and I then went to Santiago in order to
try to find him . . . that's the only thing we've lived for . . . but no one
knew anything about him. . . . Of course we turned to the officials we
knew were responsible for his and most of the other disappearances, but
there was no information to be had—not even from the churches or the
Red Cross. He simply didn't exist. It was as if he'd never existed. All
they could do was to express their sympathies. There are so many who

disappeared without a trace . . . everywhere really. (*pause*) Of course we haven't given up . . . not until we know for sure . . . you just can't.

MADELEINE H
You still think he might be alive?

ROSA
Yes. I'm sure he's alive . . . but he doesn't know who he is. . . . What else do I have to be sure of? (*short pause*) We know that most of the children of political prisoners were sent to military orphanages in the north of Chile to be cleansed of their political views, but strangely enough the military, that's usually so incredibly careful to keep the re-cords of its crimes, does not have any information about what happened to our son, Paolo.

MADELEINE H
That must be like an open wound in your life.

ROSA
Yes, yes it is. It's an open wound. . . . It was after our many trips to Chile—we've been there eleven times—that I started to write my book, a kind of conversation with him.

MADELEINE H
Let's see . . . here . . . there's a photograph of him in the book. . . . (*We see a photo of a boy, seven years old, on the TV screen. He is sitting on a simple chair with his foot in a cast. He smiles into the camera.*) There he is.

ROSA
Yes. (*looks at the picture*) There he's seven. . . . It was taken on the terrace of the children's wing at the St. Magdalena Hospital in Santiago. His right foot is in a cast. He was playing around with his dad, and his foot got stuck under one of those self-propelled "merry-go-rounds" they have in many playgrounds. . . . My husband happened to push it too hard; it must've hurt terribly. . . . We're there visiting him. . . . My husband took the picture. Our son is telling us how badly he's itching under the cast. . . . We had brought him fruit and books. He loves to read. . . . It

was in the middle of September. My husband was working at the Barros
Luco Hospital . . . had just started a project working with mental health
problems among "blue collar" workers. . . . I had just started work as a
journalist for *Punto Final*. We were both very busy, but like a miracle we
were given this last day together. . . . That was one of the last days of
freedom . . . but the air was filled with anxiety and tension. . . . Inflation
was running wild and the international banks were trying to bring Chile
down on its knees; and everyone knew that something was going to
happen. . . . Then, on September 23, we had the military coup. My husband was working . . . (*The picture of the son disappears as she is
speaking.*)

(*Eric Turns around when the answering machine picks up, but he doesn't
pick up the receiver.*)

(*Rosa continues.*) Yes . . . he's so beautiful.

MADELEINE H
(*after a short pause*) It must've been very painful to write about . . .

(*Eric's recorded voice ends.*)

ROSA
(*cuts her off*) Of course. It was like pulling myself out of my grave.

LUCA'S VOICE
(*on a telephone answering machine*) It's me again. Sorry. (*Eric lowers
the sound from the TV.*) Sorry I'm saying I'm sorry. I know you don't
like it . . . still, here I am saying it. Sometimes I have to do what I want to
do. . . . I just wanted to tell you that today I saw a woman I thought was
her . . . again. During my lunch hour. I was at *Deux Magots* when she
passed me by, walking briskly, but she glanced at me quickly, our eyes
met, incredibly quickly, but there was something in her eyes, I don't
know what, surprise maybe, her eyes opened up wide, and suddenly . . .
like time stood still, heavenly still, all sounds disappeared and I heard an
inner voice telling me, "It's her." Then it was over, and without ever
really having stopped, she started to walk again, and I got up and started
to follow her. . . . She went down to *Lemarie*, as if she didn't have a

specific destination in mind, just out window-shopping on her lunch hour. In a small boutique she tried on a pair of shoes, but wasn't sure she liked them. (*The call is interrupted.*)

MADELEINE H

Thank you so much for taking time out to come here.

ROSA

Thank you.

MADELEINE H

Thank you. (*short pause*) Now we're going to take a look at a film clip about the American artist Barton Lidice Benes, who represents a new direction in the New York art world that has emerged these last years—a kind of body-art, where the artists use their own bodies, both as materiel and ideas, in order to describe the threats against humanity and its environment, which has emerged in this time of post-industrialism and the AIDS epidemic—an art-form that to many seems to carry great similarities to the martyr-art that flourished at the end of the middle ages. Barton Lidice Benes, who was himself infected with the HIV virus some years ago, has been noticed for his cruel, strange images, for which he often uses his own blood.

LUCA'S VOICE

(*on a telephone answering machine*) She decided she didn't like them, said "Thank you" and left, then went to Fnac, and I thought "now I'll lose her;" but after a while I ran right into her in the film-music department, standing there reading the CD cover for the "*Blue Film*," and I didn't know what to say to her. I just said, "That's kitsch." And then I said "I'm sorry" and left. . . . It just can't be. Miracles like these don't happen . . . even though I'm sure it'll happen just like that. I'll see her walk by when I'm sitting in some café. She looked so much like the woman I remember, even though the woman in my memory is a woman full of laughter . . . and of course much younger. (*laughs*) Tonight is the last performance of "*Violent Nights*." Since you can't make it I'll go all by myself. . . . But Eric, call me later. Otherwise I'll die. (*laughs*) Why would it be her? Why would she be in Paris?

2.

*(Rosa and Eric have had their dinner. They are still sitting at the big din-
ing room table drinking wine.)*

ERIC

No, you were wonderful, very good, very down to earth.

ROSA

I felt terribly insecure; I became pompous and bombastic, talked as if my
life was a novel.

ERIC

It was a little shocking to see the photograph.

ROSA

You don't think I was too tense, too superficial, too obsequious? I felt I
was looking for words I don't normally use. . . . I felt like I was adver-
tising something.

ERIC

No, no, no . . . not at all. On the contrary. Do you want a piece of fruit?
(wipes his mouth, pours more wine) I just reacted the way an oyster does
when lemon juice is squeezed on it. I retracted . . . but it passed.

ROSA

The whole time I had a single sentence spinning in my head, something I
wanted to say, but I couldn't remember it. . . . Sorry, what did you say?

ERIC

I hadn't seen it . . . since we came to Paris. Remember how horrible it
was to develop the photographs? . . . No, you didn't sound pompous;
more importantly, it didn't turn too personal. You can't let it get too personal in a program like that.

ROSA

So, you don't think it was tasteless and vulgar to participate . . . to talk
about one's child?

ERIC

Not the way you did it.

ROSA

Why haven't you looked at it for twenty-two years? That's a long time. (*short pause*) It's so easy, during that moment, when you know that thousands of people are looking at you with indifferent curiosity, to try to affect them somehow. It's an intoxicating feeling, really, to try to tell it all . . . as if you'd be forgiven if you told them everything.

ERIC

There are many who do tell it all. They've made it a profession.

ROSA

(*drinks wine*) So, you've stopped thinking about him?

ERIC

How could I?

ROSA

I don't know.

ERIC

I think about him every day. (*pause*) To pull oneself . . . to pull oneself out of the grave, I think that's what you said. That was well said.

ROSA

My God! So you still think I know how to express myself, but not like when we were first married. But maybe that's because of you. (*She lifts her glass and looks into his eyes.*) Anyway, it's done, now the grave is empty. I'm smiling at you.

ERIC

Yes, and I'm smiling back.

ROSA

Yes, I see (*lightly*) as if that too, was your duty. I didn't find any shoes I liked.

ERIC

No? (*short pause*) It felt strange to be reminded of that old project with the mentally ill in *Recoleta*. It felt like something that had happened in another lifetime. I don't even know if there's anything of myself left from that time. Of course . . . almost all psychiatrists start out practicing on the poorest and the most destitute in our society, so that later, when they are more skilled, they can tackle the traumas of the middle class, which pays a great deal better. I have hundreds of photographs and films I haven't even developed yet. I documented the behavior of every patient, because at that time we believed that the illness was some kind of language that we, at some point, were going to understand, as long as there existed a loving environment. . . . Sometimes I think I've saved them because I long to end up there myself. I think that was the most important time of my life.

ROSA

Wasn't that when you met me?

ERIC

Patient and society were one. Patient and physician were one. . . . Yes, of course it was.

ROSA

We were never together. . . . We still aren't. We just discuss what we've done on any given day.

ERIC

We're together every day. We talk, eat, fall asleep . . . and wake up together.

ROSA

Don't you understand what I mean? (*pause*) Would we continue to live together if we didn't have a child that we'd lost?

ERIC

(*after a pause*) I don't know. (*pause*) What do you think?

ROSA

I don't know. I don't know anything about love.

ERIC

(*makes a joke*) Other than it's blind. Thank God, I don't want to be there the day love can see. (*pause*) Tired?

ROSA

Yes, but just because you are. But never tired enough to not be longing for you. . . . Is that a new jacket you're wearing?

ERIC

Yes. (*short pause*) Maybe a little too youthful for me, you think?

ROSA

It looks good on you, but isn't that what it's all about. (*short pause*) Tomorrow at eleven I'm supposed to be at Fnac for a book signing.

ERIC

It's Saturday. . . . I was thinking of seeing the Hosoe show tomorrow — the one who photographed Mishima.

ROSA

Aha. (*short pause*) Couldn't you wait for me? I'd love to experience a few things with you. We could go there together, and then we could walk along the river, and then maybe go someplace for a bite to eat. . . . We never do anything like that . . . like other people do. But maybe you're used to doing everything by yourself.

ERIC

No. That sounds good . . . but you really can't walk along the river these days. (*pause*) What was the sentence you couldn't remember?

ROSA

Now I remember. I wanted to change the world. I didn't want the world to change me. But it did. (*pause*) So, what are we doing this Easter?

ERIC

What are we doing this Easter?

ROSA

You're off, and I am too.

ERIC

(sighs) Uhm . . . I really don't know. I'm not really sure that I'm off. I'll
be quite busy with the final exams of the new analysts.

ROSA

What about the summer then?

ERIC

Well . . . I don't know.

ROSA

We've got to spend the summer together because this fall . . . I'm con-
sidering, but I'm not sure yet . . . but I think I'll stay in Moscow for one
more year. I can't give it up now.

ERIC

Of course you can't.

ROSA

But, if you asked me to, I would in a second. (*She puts her hand out and
he takes it. She smiles.*) I think there's a chance now . . . that we could
begin to live. Maybe because the book is finally out, out of me too. . . .
I'm free . . . as if he has grown up . . . as if I should let him live his own
life. It feels like we finally will be able to breathe. Maybe now we'll be
able to live, if not a happy life, then a life in a compromise with our loss.
(*short pause*) After all, he's twenty-seven years old! He might even have
children of his own, if he's still alive.

ERIC

"Therefore we must call no man happy while he waits to see his last day,
not until he has passed the border of life and death without suffering
pain." *Oedipus Rex.*

ROSA

That's what I said: Not happy, but maybe a compromise with happiness. (*short pause*) What do you think he's doing, what kind of work, I mean?

ERIC

I don't know . . . anything, I guess.

ROSA

Maybe he's an artist . . . or a physician . . .

ERIC

It depends on if he's forgotten us.

ROSA

What do you mean by that?

ERIC

I don't know. (*pause*) I have tickets for *Oedipus Rex* next Thursday. Can you make it?

ROSA

I'll make sure I can. . . . I wish it wasn't so easy for you to accept my being away for so long.

ERIC

One year goes very fast. (*smiles*)

ROSA

All years go fast.

ERIC

And I could come and see you some weekends here and there. . . . Don't give it up right now, when so much is happening over there.

ROSA

I'm just so tired of their suffering.

ERIC

I understand.

ROSA

There's no hope. They don't believe in anything. They plunder their own graves. They don't even have children's songs to sing, because the communists used them for their own propaganda. Here and there people try to help, try to teach illiterates to read and write. The Salvation Army has opened in St. Petersburg, but (*in a different tone of voice*) tonight I need you. I can't stand it. You know how I feel, I need it. . . . What about you?

ERIC

I don't know. One of my patients died today. He called to say good-bye. He had AIDS, below 200 T-cells, and he was blind.

ROSA

So maybe it was for the best.

ERIC

Yes.

ROSA

You can't be there for everybody. Just me. Why should you have to die as well? Please Eric . . .

ERIC

I don't know if I know what to do anymore.

ROSA

Of course you do. If I can, you can. We haven't done it for almost half a year.

ERIC

Why don't we do something else? All it does is cause pain.

ROSA

I like pain. Pain is the only thing that brings me back to a time when I could feel something. When I was able to feel something. (*folds her napkin, removes her necklace*)

3.

(Inside Luca's sparsely furnished apartment in the north part of Paris we see badly damaged old furniture, "workout" clothes, books, a computer, a large photograph of Vittorio de Sica taken in Paris in 1936, a picture of a young Katharine Hepburn and a picture of Jean Seaberg from the film "Til the Last Breath," cups and plates, CDs, folders, writing paper, note books. Luca has been changing outfits five times before the doorbell rings. He's exhausted when he finally opens the door. Music by Nina Simone is heard.)

LUCA

My God, you sure took a fucking long time! It's almost a quarter past twelve!

ERIC

That's what I said. I'll be there by twelve.

LUCA

Had it been me, I'd been here a quarter to twelve.

ERIC

Yes, but now I'm here. Don't make such a fuss.

LUCA

I'm not making a fuss. I'm just nervous.

ERIC

(He comes into the room. Luca is pacing nervously.) I'm here. *(He is carrying two shopping bags filled with gifts.)* Happy birthday!

LUCA

Please, sit down. *(He pulls Eric over to one of the dirty chairs and removes pieces of clothing hanging on it.)* Here, sit here. *(pushes Eric into the chair)*

ERIC

Take it easy.

LUCA

How could I? This has to go quickly. . . . How much time do you have? (*pulls Eric out of the chair*) No, why don't you sit over here instead. When you sit over there you look like a painting by Bacon. One hour?

ERIC

(*laughs a little*) Just take it easy. (*He takes a CD out of the bag—Sofia Gubajdulina's symphony "Stimmen . . . Verstummen."*) This is the symphony everyone's talking about. Hope you like it. What is it?

LUCA

Nina Simone.

ERIC

No, what's with you?

LUCA

Why don't you lie down on the bed instead? It's just as well. Do I get one hour? What will we have time for in an hour?

ERIC

There's a lot one can do in one hour. (*takes out a bottle of eau-detoilette*) You'll like this one.

LUCA

Please, Eric, take your clothes off. (*holds him tightly*) Take everything off. That's all I want. (*embraces him, leaves him, embraces him again*) Do you want a glass of wine? Time enough to get divorced. Is that what you want? Should we just be friends instead? Father and son?

ERIC

(*looks at his watch*) I'll have a little, not too much. Luca dear, open your presents. How are you doing?

LUCA

I think you're doing better than I am. (*He fetches the wine bottle and two glasses, drops one glass, and it breaks. Eric takes the bottle and the*

other glass from him, uncorks the wine, and pours some into the glass.)
Are you going back later?

ERIC

I have to. . . . Did you work out today?

LUCA

Honestly?

ERIC

Did you work out today?

LUCA

You think I need to? Am I getting old and flabby? Not as flabby as you though. . . . But sure, I like used bodies. How much time do I get? Are we getting together tonight?

ERIC

I'm working until nine tonight. I'm sorry.

LUCA

What about later?

ERIC

It won't work.

LUCA

So, you're here for lunch only? I'm your lunch. . . . Who do I have to talk to?

ERIC

Talk to me. (*pause*) Talk. (*short pause*) Sorry.

LUCA

So I have forty-five minutes—a therapist's hour. . . . My God, how will I have time to express everything I don't want to say in forty-five minutes?

ERIC

I can't help it; that's how it is right now.

LUCA

Will it ever get any better?

ERIC

I think so.

LUCA

Do you think I'm asking for too much? Just think how quickly we get old.

ERIC

No, no, not at all.

LUCA

I'd like to be able to walk with you and be with you just like other lovers, walk along the river, sit on some park bench. I don't even need to hold your hand, as long as I know you're there and won't disappear the next moment. Maybe we could go to a movie, or sit at some bar and talk openly and freely . . . without constraints. . . . Have ordinary, comfortable conversations, ordinary, comfortable times together that won't feel like I'm stealing you from your other existence. We haven't even been to the movies, even though we've been together for a whole year!

ERIC

You can't walk along the river anymore. . . . I know. I'm sorry. That's what I want too. There are a few more gifts. Why don't you open them?

LUCA

Why? I don't need a dad who doesn't have time for me but gives me money instead. Thank you. What is it? *(Eric gives him the gift.)*

ERIC

A novel by Thomas Bernhard.

LUCA

How boring. (*walks back and forth in the room, doesn't open the gift*) Am I supposed to be sitting here reading while you're fucking her? (*short pause*) Today we did a lung autopsy. A forty-nine year old taxi driver. It smelled like slaughter-house and nicotine. Are you going to talk to her?

ERIC

Yes.

LUCA

When?

ERIC

Now. Soon. I'm waiting for the right moment, a moment that's right for both of us.

LUCA

Does a moment like that really exist? What will happen then?

ERIC

I don't know . . . maybe she'll die.

LUCA

You think so? (*pause*) Do you think? (*short pause*) From what? How?

ERIC

I'll talk to her during our vacation, when we're both rested. I'll spend our vacation explaining, deal with tears, suffer and separate together.

LUCA

So, I'll be alone this summer too? Then what?

ERIC

I think I owe her that.

LUCA

What about me, what do you owe me?

ERIC

And that I'm with her when I tell her I'm leaving, even though I'm
probably the last one who could or should try to help her. But we've
lived together for thirty years, we share a country we can't return to, we
share a lost child we'll never find—together we've experienced expectation and hope and repression, incarceration and emigration . . .

LUCA

How the hell could I compete with that? You don't even give me a
chance to experience anything with you . . . except death, maybe . . .
AIDS.

ERIC

We're the parents of a son who's neither dead nor alive—just lost. I'm
both her heaven and hell. I have to leave her in a way that'll harm her as
little as possible and will give her hope that I'm there for her, until she,
herself, realizes that it's meaningless.

LUCA

She's so beautiful that maybe tomorrow she'll meet someone who'll
make her happy. Would that make you unhappy? Do you regret meeting
me? Do you regret that day?

ERIC

No. Of course I do, now and then . . .

LUCA

You'll never have to regret it, once you really know me.

ERIC

The first time we met, which was also the first time we made love, was
in my student apartment in Santiago. Afterwards she said to me that if I
ever left her, she would die like an abandoned animal.

LUCA

Yes, you two really belong to a melodramatic generation. Such bullshit.
Isn't it wonderful to be loved like this . . . having the power over two
lives?

ERIC

We've only known each other for half a year.

LUCA

One year.

ERIC

Half a year.

LUCA

In a physical sense, yes. But when I started my analysis I entered into—you were the one who seduced me—a relationship with you; the other stuff is just physical. (*pause*) I could use someone to talk to. (*starts to laugh*) I could use a therapist. I could use you. Since you're the best therapist there is. A better therapist than lover anyway. . . . After you there's no other therapist to go to. (*He keeps moving around in the room, removes books and papers from the only chair, and pulls Eric up to the window and then back again while he's talking.*) Do you want some other kind of music?

ERIC

You can't go on living like this.

LUCA

I can, but you can't. You're just visiting poverty. It's easier when you get used to it.

ERIC

(*calmly*) I think I've known worse poverty and misery than you.

LUCA

(*aggressively*) What do you know about it? Well, I'm sorry, I forgot that you know everything. (*Now the music consists solely of drums being played very loudly.*) You, who can easily spend three hundred dollars for a shirt without thinking twice . . . and your wife probably spends ten thousand dollars for summer dresses every year.

ERIC

(*makes a face*) Please turn it down a little.

LUCA

Anyway, when you're both dead you won't have any more than those newborn corpses they find in the lockers at *Gare du Nord*. . . . I really don't understand how one can buy things. Every time you do, it must remind you that death will take it all away.

ERIC

I was just thinking of this place.

LUCA

I like it here. This is my home. We've got to take care of what we have, because this is all we'll ever have.

ERIC

(*referring to an iron floor lamp with rusty metal shade*) That's a nice lamp.

LUCA

Do you want it?

ERIC

No . . . then you won't have any light.

LUCA

I don't need to see. I keep my eyes closed most of the time. That one would look like a skinhead in your apartment; of course, I haven't seen it. . . . My whole life is in pieces, but you, you just live like before, exactly like before, right? Nothing has happened to your life. It's exactly the way it was, right? Am I right? (*He lights a cigarette, walks up to Eric and embraces him. They hug and caress each other.*) Come, let's at least lie down. (*He starts to unbutton Eric's shirt and pulls off his jacket.*)

ERIC

You can't remove my shirt before my jacket. . . . Do you really think we should? (*looks around, the window has no curtains*) There are people over there, across the street. . . . Everybody can see us.

LUCA

Just relish it. (*He pulls him down onto the bed, facing each other.*) Did you go back to your dull sex life with her?

ERIC

No.

LUCA

But you're going to?

ERIC

No . . . I don't think so. . . . I can't.

LUCA

Doesn't she miss it? (*pause*) Answer me.

ERIC

We're working all the time. Don't talk about that now. (*Luca stands up and puts on a different CD.*) Why are you getting up?

LUCA

I want you to listen to this one.

ERIC

I don't want her to die . . . that's all.

LUCA

Listen, listen . . . (*The music is* "The Wind" *with Keith Jarrett.*) Do you think she will?

ERIC

Yes, I do. (*sits up*) I have a strange notion that I could leave her without her noticing. (*Luca turns up the volume of the music.*) As if I'd just died—not because I'd met someone else, and a man at that . . . young enough to be her son. (*short pause*) I have to give her something to live for, before I leave her. . . . I'm the last man in her life.

LUCA

I saw her on TV last night. She's beautiful.

ERIC

Yes. Very beautiful.

LUCA

She doesn't look forty-nine. I couldn't hear everything she said. She seems cold.

ERIC

Losing something can make you cold.

LUCA

I've lost something too.

ERIC

Me too.

LUCA

The difference is that you can live with it.

ERIC

Do you still have nightmares?

LUCA

Only when I'm awake. . . . That's why I came to you. Who the hell can I go to now?

ERIC

I'll ask around. The only thing is that the good ones are almost impossible to get to see. (*short pause*) Don't you remember anything about your parents . . . the feeling in your home, what it looked like where you lived . . . some kind of emotional connection?

LUCA

You know damn well I don't.

ERIC

Of course you do, but you can't get to it.

LUCA

Same thing. My life starts in the prison. Before that there's no life. The guards give me chocolate and comic books—Donald Duck and Spider-man—and at night they rape me. There are three of them. Two of them are kind of nice and young, always laughing and kidding around, but the third one, the older one, he always cries afterwards and begs for for-giveness. (*short pause*) In the beginning I was in a cell with some people my own age. One of them had his mother there with him, and they forced him . . . to torture her. What do say to that? You, who've heard everything.

ERIC

Of course that's very traumatic, terribly traumatic, but a trauma doesn't always have to remain a trauma; it can be transformed into becoming an important part of one's personality.

LUCA

I don't give a fuck about that. I don't give a fuck about my personality. I just want to find my parents. No, I'm not sure about that either. . . . I want to know who they are and where they are. Doesn't matter if they're dead or alive, as long as I find out their names.

ERIC

On one level you'll have to accept them as dead.

LUCA

I just want a gravesite. I need a grave.

ERIC

Yes. (*short pause*) I know it must be terrible. (*sits up*) I'm still wearing my shoes. Sorry.

LUCA

I want to make love. . . . That's the only thing that makes me forget.

ERIC

I can't . . . not now.

LUCA

Don't worry. I still have a condom. . . . American.

ERIC

Have you been with an American?

LUCA

What am I to do?

ERIC

Where?

LUCA

Where? What does it matter? (*short pause*) In the Russian Embassy.

ERIC

When? When did it happen?

LUCA

What does it matter? I need a little human contact . . . with anyone, now and then.

ERIC

Who was it? Someone you knew?

LUCA

Of course not, I don't make love to people I know. That's so boring. It was an American soldier, a black guy. I like soldiers. My background, you know.

ERIC

You've got to be careful.

LUCA

I like them because they know what they want. . . . I was totally spent afterwards. He almost killed me. (*short pause*) The guys I like the most are those who do things they never thought they would do; it makes them brutal.

ERIC

You're the one being brutal to yourself.

LUCA

That's the most thrilling moment, the spotlight in your face, paralyzed like a deer. You don't know what's coming.

ERIC

You could get infected.

LUCA

I could get killed. I'm already infected. (*short pause*) What does it matter?

ERIC

What makes you say that?

LUCA

Does that frighten you?

ERIC

No. . . . Yes, of course it does.

LUCA

Poor Eric. . . . You, who've got so much to live for. Your wife, your apartment, all the poor, unhappy people you give comfort to. . . . Maybe we'll have two or three romantic years together before everything comes to an end.

ERIC

Well, that's enough.

LUCA

For you, maybe. (*pulls him down*) Spend a little time with me while I'm still warm . . . then you can secretly spread my ashes somewhere. Put them in a small box with the others at *Gare du Nord.* After that you can go on with your life.

4.

(*Rosa and Eric are coming home late at night to their apartment. They are all dressed up.*)

ERIC

(*while helping her take off her coat*) How wonderful that when we finally had time to go to the theater we saw such a great production. Although all that traffic tires me out. . . . I don't know how much longer one can go on living here.

ROSA

Yes . . . I guess.

ERIC

(*while the coat glides out of his hands*) But the subject is always interesting, bloody and interesting. Every time I see him searching for the evidence of his own total destruction I get just as frightened . . . and yet not . . . because he, although blind, is moving towards a more truthful existence. (*laughs*) I identify with all three characters.

ROSA

While you're getting my coat all dirty. . . . You dropped it (*points*) over there.

ERIC

I'm sorry. (*picks it up*) Who did you identify with?

ROSA

Who do you want me to identify with? Are you tired?

ERIC

Being human, that's all . . . but just like that, stripped naked like a skeleton, like it was in this production, bare boned. Hardly ever do we get insights like that. Only in the theater can horror beautifully and artistically portrayed seem like reconciliation. . . . I don't understand why my patients don't take the opportunity to scream and cry more than they do?

ROSA

I asked if you're tired.

ERIC

Yes, I guess I am . . . but only deep down. (*He walks into the room and turns on the lights.*) No one lives here. . . . Do you want a glass of wine?

ROSA

We live here. . . . Tired of what?

ERIC

It was a short play. We've got the whole evening left . . . but truth is always short.

ROSA

Does it feel like we have too much time? Don't you know what to do with me for that many hours? What makes you so tired?

ERIC

Just that so many people need me.

ROSA

Am I one of them too?

ERIC

(*somewhat sharply*) No, of course not. (*pours some wine, gives her a glass*) How did it go at Fnac?

ROSA

I don't remember. Thank you. (*remembers*) We forgot to vote.

ERIC

My God, who would we vote for? This country is just the sum of its obsessions. Also, we're strangers here, it's not our country. We're al-

lowed to stay here only as long as we don't demand anything or make
ourselves heard. . . . And that suits me fine.

ROSA

(*drinks*) I think I wrote my name maybe a hundred and sixty times, until
I forgot how to spell it.

ERIC

I've a feeling I'm done here.

ROSA

Most people were just passing by, but maybe there'll be someone who'll
read the book.

ERIC

I'm sure.

ROSA

When will you read it?

ERIC

Soon.

ROSA

Since it is about you.

ERIC

About me?

ROSA

(*after a long pause*) The day you understand that I love you, I'll have the
courage to hate you. (*pause*) There was a very nice young man there who
helped me, and told me when to take a break, and who brought me
mineral water and fruit. He had put a rose on my table. I talked to him a
little afterwards. Italian or Spanish. He spoke in a very wonderful and
dark French.

ERIC

Aha. Didn't you ask where he came from?

ROSA

I was going to, but I forgot. He was just a temp worker. (*takes his hand*) I
miss you. (*short pause*) And my body misses you too.

ERIC

Yeah. (*sighs, kisses her cheek*) You're so beautiful. That color really
suits you.

ROSA

Yes, I know. . . . Don't you miss me? Doesn't your body miss mine?

ERIC

Sure.

ROSA

(*after a short pause*) Do you know what he told me?

ERIC

Who?

ROSA

The young Italian or Spaniard at Fnac.

ERIC

No . . . what did he tell you?

ROSA

He said he knew you. He said, I know your husband.

ERIC

Really? . . . How strange. . . . What's his name?

ROSA

He's a patient. Seems he's been in analysis with you for some time . . .
but that you'd broken off the analysis.

ERIC

That I'd broken off? Why?

ROSA

But he said that it was probably his fault.

ERIC

Maybe we hadn't really started. . . . What's his name?

ROSA

I told you, I don't know. Hugo, I think. All your patients seem to be named Hugo.

ERIC

(*curtly*) I don't remember. (*calmer*) Who could it be?

ROSA

I told you! Young, about twenty-five, twenty-six, beautiful Southern European. Nice and well-spoken. White shirt and a leather jacket. Good looking. Unpretentious or incredibly pretentious. Difficult to say.

ERIC

When did I see him?

ROSA

He said that it wasn't your fault that the treatments had been interrupted. He thought that his problems were too simple to be worth your while.

ERIC

Wait. (*pause*) Now I know who you're thinking about. I know who you mean. Yes, that's right. (*short pause*) A little more wine?

ROSA

Yes, please, it's a good wine. Thank you. (*pause*) Why did you interrupt the analysis?

ERIC

Let's not think about him anymore.

ROSA

I'm not thinking of him. . . . I just want to know why.

ERIC

I think, because I didn't think I could help him.

ROSA

With what?

ERIC

Whatever he came to see me about.

ROSA

What was it?

ERIC

What does it matter?

ROSA

You mean you can't help everybody?

ERIC

I can only give them the possibility of looking for something of value within themselves. If it's there, or if they want to search for it, that's for them to decide. (*short pause*) Now I remember. . . . He was the one who had something wrong with his foot. He came to me because he had a feeling he was losing control over himself. He had suddenly, without knowing why, committed rather grave acts of violence against total strangers; he'd beaten an older woman in a Metro station, abused a taxi driver . . . things like that. He'd been sent to jail for a couple of months. What really freaked him out was that he had no recollection of what he'd done, and why. . . . Had forgotten everything about his childhood as well. We got as far as establishing the fact that he had repressed a major part of his childhood. He knew nothing about where he came from. I think he'd been brought up in an orphanage. If you drastically change your environment as a child, you might react by both wiping out the past, which you've lost anyway, as well as the present, which you don't want to live in.

ROSA

Very sad.

ERIC

He was studying medicine, I think. . . . It would require very long and deep therapy in order to get to the root of his problems, and I can't really accept any new patients. You know I'm trying to cut down. . . . I've had it. (*short pause*) What else did he say?

ROSA

We just talked for a short while. He was so kind. I can't imagine him being violent. . . . He was both courteous and cultured.

ERIC

I guess that's his way of keeping his aggressions at bay.

ROSA

Let's not talk anymore.

ERIC

You're the one talking.

ROSA

(*caresses the inside of his thigh*) What am I to do? I miss you. That's the truth.

ERIC

Me or it?

ROSA

It's the same thing. . . . Don't you want to?

ERIC

Yes, no, I don't know.

ROSA

You can't live without it either.

ERIC

The pain I feel is greater than the pleasure I get from it.

ROSA

Who's feeling the most pain? Who gets the most pleasure from it? So, who's feeling the most pain?

ERIC

How can you talk about pain when no one gets hurt?

ROSA

That's not true. It has never been without pain. You, who believe that if we could talk about everything we could also tell the truth . . . don't you know that there are certain thoughts you shouldn't have, because if you do, you open the gates to hell . . . and then you get used to entering, and disappearing. That's what I want. To disappear into your blazing hot fire.

ERIC

Why don't we just stop this? (*short pause*) Stop it!

ROSA

No, we can't. (*short pause*) Just think if it is the only thing uniting us these days, the only thing that's left. . . . Where would we find someone else who would understand?

ERIC

There are so many . . . every new day, more and more, children of Oedipus . . . children of Jocasta.

ROSA

Come on, let's do it. Don't wait. You like it, when you're doing it.

ERIC

You like me when I'm doing it. Do I have to?

ROSA

Yes.

(*Eric stands up, walks out of the room, and comes back carrying an old, beat-up aluminum chair, tools to tie her up with, a rusty floor lamp without a shade, and a dirty sack. Then he brings a mattress covered with cowhides, brown and stiff. He prepares the strange room, turns the lights out, turns on the rusty lamp, and walks over to her. She has her eyes closed. He puts his hand softly on her shoulder. She stands up and he, with his hand against her back, gently moves her into the part of the room he has prepared for her. He points to the chair and makes it clear that she is supposed to sit down. She sits, still with her eyes closed.*)

ERIC

Take a look. (*She opens her eyes.*)

ROSA

Good.

ERIC

(*hits her*) Shut up.

ROSA

I'm sorry.

ERIC

You don't have my permission to talk. (*He kicks her hard with his foot. It hurts and she cries out.*) Didn't you hear what I said? Not a sound from your fucking mouth. (*She bends her head down.*) Lift your head up. (*He forces her head up.*) Hurry up. . . . (*friendly*) How are you?

ROSA

Sorry.

ERIC

I said, how are you?

ROSA

I don't know.

ERIC

You don't know how you are?

ROSA

I'm sorry.

ERIC

(*still friendly*) Don't tell me you're sorry, you little Jew whore! Just answer the questions. All my questions. Then you can say you're sorry.

ROSA

Yes.

ERIC

So . . .

ROSA

(*quietly*) The music.

ERIC

(*grabs her hair, pulls her backwards*) Don't you hear what I'm telling you?

ROSA

(*quietly, faintly*) The music . . . you're forgetting the music.

ERIC

(*twists her hair slowly*) I'm not forgetting anything.

ROSA

No.

ERIC

Who's the one here who's forgetting? (*hits her face*)

ROSA

Not my face.

ERIC

Sorry.

ROSA

I have to have it.

ERIC

Why do you want it? (*He rips her blouse open, it tears, then he rips off her bra.*) This is what you like, right? (*She doesn't answer.*) Answer me. (*She doesn't answer.*) Answer me, I said. I said, you like it, don't you?

ROSA

Yes.

ERIC

So you think you're beautiful. You're wrong. You aren't beautiful. You're too old. Here we have young, beautiful girls with young firm breasts. Yours are flabby and full of veins. Who wants them? (*He's holding one of her nipples.*) Like an old tire. Who wants it? Do you think I want to be here with you? Answer me!

ROSA

No.

ERIC

Louder.

ROSA

No.

ERIC

I don't think so either. We can make this easy or hard, right? (*pause*) What would you like? Do you want it easy or hard, you old Jewish cunt?

ROSA

Yes.

ERIC

You can tell the truth, or not tell the truth. I don't give a fuck. You mean nothing to me. It doesn't matter if you're dead or alive. You don't exist. (*pulls the dirty sack over her head*) What's your name? What was your name before you came here? (*She says something.*) Louder!

ROSA

Sabato. (*short pause*) Rosa Sabato.

ERIC

Were you a Jew?

ROSA

Yes.

ERIC

So, what are you now? (*He walks over to the CD player and starts a CD with quacking ducks. At times the quacking is very loud, at other times it sounds like singing.*) Was the whole group made up of Jews only?

ROSA

I don't know . . . it wasn't a group . . . we were just students.

(*Eric hits her.*)

5.

(*Eric is in the apartment tidying up, listening to music, preparing for his work. The door intercom is heard.*)

ERIC

(*walks over and picks up the receiver*) Yes? Hello?

LUCA

(*upset*) I've got to see you! Open the door! Hurry up!

ERIC

No, I can't . . . It's not possible. (*short pause*) Please leave.

LUCA

I have to see you!

ERIC

You can't come here. You understand that, don't you? (*short pause*) Luca, go home.

LUCA

Let me in, it's important. I've got to see you right now!

ERIC

Rosa will be here any moment . . . don't you understand that? It's impossible.

LUCA

Open the door.

ERIC

I can't. It's impossible. I'll call you. (*hangs up, stays by the door, again it rings*)

LUCA

(*when Eric picks up*) I might be HIV positive. . . . What will you do then?

ERIC

No, you're not.

LUCA

What will you do? What'll you do then?

ERIC

Please, Luca . . . I can't talk to you about it on the intercom.

LUCA

You aren't giving me any other alternative! (*pause*) Am I right? (*pause*) Hello!

ERIC

Yes . . . I'm still here, but I can't talk any longer.

LUCA

Go to hell. (*pause*) Open the door! Open, I said.

ERIC

Right now I can't. I'll meet you at your place . . . (*looks at his watch*) in about three hours. (*pause*) Hello . . . I'll be there in three hours. (*silence*) Luca. (*is listening*) Luca . . . answer me. (*silence*) Luca, I know you're there. Hello . . . but answer me then. (*He waits for a while, hangs up, then lifts up the receiver again.*) I know you're there. Why don't you go home and wait for me? . . . I'll be there in three hours, at nine o'clock. Then we'll talk. (*He hangs up, walks into the living room, is extremely upset, walks over to his desk, sits down, then stands up. The doorbell rings. He runs out to the hallway, and opens the door quickly.*) What the hell is going on?

LUCA

(*quietly*) I had to see you. I just wanted to see you. Don't be afraid.

ERIC

(*after a pause*) Please leave. (*pause*) I beg you to leave.

LUCA

I just want to see how you live, how you are. (*smiles*) I was worried about you.

ERIC

Please leave. She'll be here any moment. Don't you understand?

LUCA

Isn't it just as well? Can't be good for you to be lying the whole time, to both me and her. (*He walks into the apartment.*) Yes, it looks exactly the way I imagined it would. Nice and clean . . . inhuman. Here you could live for all eternity. . . . Here you can live happily in your mausoleum. Did you know that when I visited the Uffizi Palace in Florence the first time I thought that those big coffins were bathtubs?

ERIC

Luca, I beg you.

LUCA

That's nice, that you're begging me. I'm usually the one begging you.
Why did you give me the Thomas Bernhard book? It's basically all about
suicides. . . . Do you want me to commit suicide? Is that your master
plan? (*He stomps around the room, pulls things down, throws books, and
turns over the cabinet with CDs.*)

ERIC

Stop it! Stop it! Calm down.

LUCA

Why don't you calm me down then? You're the therapist! You know
how to calm people down! (*pokes Eric in the ribs*) Come on! Why don't
you do a little therapy on me?

ERIC

(*quietly*) What is it that you want?

LUCA

What is that I want? I forgot. I want you to acknowledge me. I want you
to live with me. (*tries to embrace Eric*)

ERIC

(*pushes him away*) You aren't allowed here. (*Luca starts to get undressed, first taking off his shirt and then his pants and socks. Eric tries
to stop his actions, but Luca sits down on a chair by the desk, which is
situated by a pair of open windows, lights a cigarette, then puts his head
on the desk and is very still.*) What do you mean by all this?

LUCA

Take your clothes off. . . . I'm staying here.

ERIC

Get out of here! (*He pulls the chair out from under him and hits him.*)
Take your goddamn clothes and get out of here. (*Luca laughs.*) Get the

hell out! Get out! Get lost! Out you go! (*He pulls him through the room. Luca is trying to fight back while laughing hysterically. Eric throws him out into the hallway, fetches his clothing, throws everything out the door, then tries to throw Luca out the same way.*)

LUCA

(*still laughing*) Wow, you really are angry. . . . I didn't think you could get this angry!

ERIC

Get up and leave!

LUCA

For God's sake.

ERIC

Get out, I said.

LUCA

I can't . . . I can't walk. My foot, I can't stand on it.

ERIC

Now you've got to leave. (*calmer*) Sorry, I didn't mean to hurt you.

LUCA

I can't stand on my foot.

ERIC

Get dressed and go downstairs and I'll call for a cab.

LUCA

It's not your fault. I always have problems with my right foot. It's been broken several times. . . . By the way, my last memory of my parents is in the hospital, because I had a broken foot. I don't know how it happened, but they were there visiting me. (*He stands up slowly, rests on his left foot, and holds on to a chair.*) They brought me a lot of fruit and books. I think it was a Sunday, because the church bells kept ringing, and the weather was beautiful, so they wheeled me out on a balcony. *The*

Three Musketeers . . . never had the chance to finish it anyway. That's my last memory of them. After that they no longer exist. (*He is about to hug and kiss Eric.*) I'm so sorry, but suddenly, today, I got the answer. I am HIV-positive. I felt desperate.

ERIC

(*makes a move backwards*) No.

LUCA

It's a bitch.

ERIC

It can't be true.

LUCA

Yes, it is true. Last night I had a dream I got a letter stating that I was HIV-positive. I felt so happy when I realized it was just a dream. Then I went to a couple of classes, and when I returned home in the afternoon there was the letter from the hospital.

6.

(*In Luca's apartment, Luca is worried and can't sit still. He walks over to the telephone, calls Eric, hangs up, turns on some music, then turns it off, walks over to the closet, searches for some clothes, throws himself on the bed, gets a little calmer, and decides to get dressed and go out. The doorbell rings. Luca excitedly runs to the door in the belief that Eric has arrived, feeling both happiness and anger.*)

LUCA

So there you are! (*opens the door*)

ROSA

(*remains outside the door*) Sorry . . . sorry to disturb you this late at night. I don't know if you remember me. I saw you down in the Metro, and I thought . . . but maybe you . . .

LUCA

(*suddenly very polite*) Please, come in . . . of course I remember you. Of course . . . I didn't know . . . please, come in, the place is a real mess . . . I . . . I'm a student . . . I'm studying medicine. I think I already told you that, when we met at Fnac, but . . . well, I don't really have the time . . . or the money . . . but please come in . . .

ROSA

Thank you. I'm just . . . I don't know why I . . . well, to be honest, I'm just following some kind of impulse and . . .

LUCA

This is great, I love people who follow their impulses . . . break out of their personal prisons. . . . Not that I mean that you're in some kind of prison.

ROSA

Well, maybe I am.

LUCA

Please, come in. . . . There should be something to sit on. . . . You never think you'll meet someone you've just met here in Paris, someone you don't know very well . . . someone you've been thinking about; but, on the other hand, you could say the complete opposite—only in Paris do you meet someone you've been thinking about but don't know at all. . . . Do you live in the neighborhood?

ROSA

No, no.

LUCA

Do you live in the center of the city?

ROSA

Pretty much. . . . I feel I have to for my work.

LUCA

The eighth?

ROSA

No. Not on *Champs-Élysées*. (*laughs a little*)

LUCA

(*He has just lit a cigarette.*) I'm sorry . . . is it all right? (*extinguishes the cigarette*) Well . . .

ROSA

No, no . . . it's fine . . . please smoke your cigarette. . . . Do you live alone?

LUCA

Yes. . . . No. I'm always with people. I like being all alone among people. Today I performed a post-mortem on a human. (*short pause*) In the beginning I couldn't look as I was about to cut, but the pathologist said, "You'll get used to it" . . . and that was true. (*She looks at him and their eyes meet. He smiles quickly, then turns away and looks down.*) Yes . . . you're married. . . . Sure, your husband . . . what did he say? (*laughs*) Did he remember me . . . or my symptoms? . . . Does he remember a man who doesn't remember?

ROSA

Yes . . . oh, yes. (*short pause*) I really don't know why I came here.

LUCA

No, but you wish it would happen more often, don't you think? (*stands up*) That you meet someone who . . . who you don't have to explain anything to. And then . . . why don't you stand up? (*Rosa stands up. Luca embraces her, kisses her.*)

ROSA

And then?

LUCA

(*He unbuttons her blouse and caresses her breasts. They undress each other then make love. They lay side by side holding hands, not looking at each other. After a while Luca smiles.*) You usually don't smoke after making love?

ROSA

I usually never smoke . . . but you can smoke, if you want to.

LUCA

No, I don't want to. (*pause*) I'm completely satisfied. (*longer pause*) Did you have time to catch Chéreaus' film, "Queen Margot?"

ROSA

No, no, haven't seen anything. . . . There's so much I haven't had time to see.

LUCA

The critics seemed bewildered. . . . There's a fantastic scene at the end where the queen-mother, Verna Lisi, burns her underwear. She has syphilis. She's rotting from within. Her face looks like a cranium. . . . Adjani plays Margot.

ROSA

Yes, I have to see it. I'll try to see it.

LUCA

Yes. There isn't enough time for everything. (*pause*) Did you like it?

ROSA

Yes. I think so.

LUCA

But a lot depends on your motive . . . am I right?

ROSA

What motive did I have?

LUCA

The same as mine maybe. (*pause*) Punishment?

ROSA

I've never done this before. (*short pause*) Where are you from?

LUCA

(*short pause*) What do you mean? You don't think I'm French?

ROSA

No, please, don't take it the wrong way. (*pause*) But you aren't, are you?

LUCA

No, what am I then? (*sits up, looks at her*) Do you want something to drink?

ROSA

No, thanks. (*sits up as well, looking around for her clothes*) Spain?

LUCA

Spain? No, not Spain.

ROSA

(*after a pause*) It could be anywhere.

LUCA

Yes . . . anywhere. (*He stands up, fetches her bra, and gives it to her. She is sitting like a little girl, with her hands between her thighs.*)

ROSA

It's almost more embarrassing getting dressed than undressed the first time.

LUCA

(*about to put on his socks*) Did you make love to me because I used to be your husband's patient?

ROSA

(*starts to laugh*) No, not at all. . . . I don't think so. (*notices his injured foot*) What happened? What did you do to your foot?

LUCA

I saw you on TV the other day, when you were being interviewed. . . . I thought you looked so beautiful, but I couldn't hear what you said. My TV sound disappears after a while.

ROSA

What happened to your foot?

LUCA

Nothing . . . I broke it when I was little, and obviously I didn't get great care.

ROSA

How? (*pause*) What had happened? (*louder*) How did it happen?

LUCA

Why do you ask?

ROSA

How long . . . how long have you lived in Paris?

LUCA

Well . . . I've lived here . . . I came here in the spring of '89. (*lights a cigarette*) I'm studying medicine. I'm going to become a physician. I've been studying for two-and-a-half years. I plan to become a general practitioner . . . meet regular people.

ROSA

Who are you? (*after a short pause*) Are your parents alive?

LUCA

My parents? Sure . . . I hope so . . . I mean, I haven't had much to do with them this last year. They're so far away. My dad is an insurance salesman for an American company in Santiago.

ROSA

American?

LUCA

He's fifty-eight years old. He's beginning to talk about retirement. We don't have that much in common, really . . . like most fathers and sons. He loves to play soccer, is always doing athletic stuff . . . likes hiking in the mountains, goes fishing . . . all those things. He has adopted some kind of American lifestyle. My mom is a teacher. I have no siblings. (*looks at her*) What's going on? Don't you feel well?

ROSA

I'm . . . I'm OK.

LUCA

That said, they're my foster parents . . . I'm adopted . . .

ROSA

(*after a long pause, barely audible*) And your other . . . the other . . .

LUCA

Who?

ROSA

Your real parents . . . where are . . .

LUCA

They aren't very real. Only biological. . . . He's very much to the right, an admirer of Pinochet. If he were an American he'd vote for Ross Perot.

ROSA

Where are they? . . . What happened to them? . . . What do you know?

LUCA

My biological parents? (*pause*) I don't know. (*lightly*) Dead, maybe. They were so young. They disappeared during the military coup. They were socialists. (*lights a cigarette*) I guess you know everything about all that.

ROSA

No . . . no.

LUCA

I guess I was six or seven when it happened. . . . I'd just started school. All I have is a hazy memory of two beautiful, obscure characters. . . . She was so happy and full of life. . . . Dark, short hair . . .

ROSA

No. (*long pause*) No.

LUCA

(*who is now almost fully dressed*) But those things happened . . .

(*They hear the door being opened. Luca reacts with horror. Rosa is sitting frozen on the bed. Eric enters.*)

7.

(*Eric comes in through the door, the key still in his hand. The room is in semi- darkness.*)

ERIC

Luca. (*He notices Rosa sitting on the bed with her head bent down, staring at nothing, while wringing her hands. Luca is standing in the middle of the room, frozen, looking the way he did before the door opened, with an expression of astonishment, malicious delight, and expectation. Eric looks at Luca who is looking at Rosa. She doesn't want to see either one of them. Eric then looks at the key in his hand, squeezes it, and turns his head away. There is a long silence.*)

LUCA

Well . . . What's there to say? (*short pause*) What does one usually say in a situation like this? . . . One could say that it is in fucking bad taste to drop in like this, without any warning, but then again, isn't that the risk the intruder takes? And maybe it's just as well. The truth always wins out, sooner or later. Maybe this came to light a little bit too late. . . . Honesty always wins . . . but . . . (*laughs*) I don't know if I can offer you something to eat or drink, when I've just been fucking your wife. . . . It's a pity we had to meet like this, in this pig sty, since the three of us have so much in common. . . . But like Bourdieu says—I can't resist quoting him—our biggest problem is that we've ended up in the wrong place; it's no longer "*condition humaine*" but "*position humaine*" that is agonizing to us. . . . And it's getting cold in here. (*to Rosa*) Are you cold? The super's wife drinks, and so does he. . . . Well, you know how it is. No use talking about everything now; it'll take too long—deceit, bad conscience, dirt and filth, repetition and acceptance. It happened. It's better that the two of you go to a center for family counseling, or maybe that you do something good for the heroin addicts from North Africa.

ROSA

(*She is getting dressed. Eric is avoiding looking at her. Luca tries to be courteous and helpful, but she doesn't react. She stands up, walks around, and stops by a photograph of Eric standing in a square in Florence.*) I took that picture last summer in Florence. (*short pause*) I never saw it before.

LUCA

I went there for a week, hoping that we suddenly would bump into each other somewhere and maybe have an espresso together. . . . Isn't it a nice picture? (*short pause*) It's a happy picture.

ROSA

We were talking about going back this summer, for a couple of weeks, to the same place.

LUCA

Too bad we had to meet like this the first time, but . . . shit happens.

ROSA

(*doesn't turn around*) This isn't the first time.

LUCA

Sorry?

ROSA

(*whispers*) This isn't the first time.

LUCA

I mean, the three of us. This is the first time the three of us are together.

ROSA

We've been together before.

LUCA

Really? . . . Where? (*aggressively towards Eric*) For God's sake, sit down, do something! (*in a different tone of voice*) I don't remember that. Where?

ROSA

(*She looks at Luca, then, finally, at Eric.*) You are my son.

LUCA

Sorry? (*smiles*)

ROSA

You are my son, our son. You are our son. You are Paolo, our son. The last time I saw you, you were in the hospital in 1974. You were seven years old. It was on a Sunday. You were there because you had a broken foot, and Eric and I came to see you. It was on a Sunday. We brought you fruit and books . . . because you liked to read. . . . We were on the balcony. It was on a Sunday.

LUCA

You already said that.

ROSA

That was the last time I saw you.

LUCA

No. No. (*laughs*) Not me.

ROSA

That was the last time I saw you.

LUCA

No, no, no, that wasn't me. It couldn't have been me. (*short pause*) What book? What book? What books?

ROSA

It's true.

LUCA

What books, I said.

ROSA

It is true.

ERIC

Yes.

LUCA

Aha . . . (*short pause*) So, what are you going to do now?

ERIC

I don't know. . . . I didn't know. . . . How could I know?

LUCA

That's no excuse.

ROSA

How are you going to go on living? . . . We?

ERIC

(*screams for the first time*) I can't!

LUCA

What about me? What will happen to me . . . with parents like you? It can't be true. . . . I'll never be able to meet other people. . . . How will I be able to meet other people and tell them . . . about my parents?

ERIC

I didn't know. . . . How would I . . . how could I . . .

ROSA

No.

ERIC

He was just a patient . . . anyone . . .

ROSA

I can't stay here. (*sits down*) It feels like I've lost all my blood.

LUCA

That's terrible . . . that must feel terrible.

ROSA

(*She stands up again, looking around for a door.*) I want to leave.

LUCA

(*quietly*) There's no place to go.

ERIC

(*to himself*) Is it still a crime if you didn't know you committed it?

LUCA

(*to Rosa*) Take it easy. . . . Do sit down.

ERIC

Either we have to . . . stay together and help each other through this . . . or just go . . . each in a different direction, and never see each other again.

ROSA

My husband and my son . . . my husband and my son . . . my husband and my son . . .

ERIC

I didn't know what I was doing.

ROSA

My husband and my son, my husband and my son.

ERIC

What about you? (*pause*) We can't talk about this? . . . Do you understand?

ROSA

What are we to do?

LUCA

There's only one thing to do.

EPILOGUE

In a cell for two people, which is quite homey looking, half is occupied by a camera crew readying themselves for a TV interview. Luca is sitting on a chair, smiling pleasantly. He seems humble, calm, with no strong emotions showing, as if he is psychologically cleansed. The cell, which contains books, toiletries, a transistor radio, and two beds, has a normal-size, iron-grid-covered window. We can't really make out the landscape outside the window, but it seems flat, walled in. Luca is wearing his own clothes—a shirt, pants, and summer shoes. In the corner behind Madeleine Hirsch is the cameraman holding a video camera, a sound technician, and a grip. All of them are in control of the situation.

MADELEINE H

(*to the cameraman*) Whenever you're ready we'll start.

CAMERAMAN

We're ready. (*short pause*) Just one more little thing.

MADELEINE H

OK, thank you. (*to Luca*) You always have to wait. (*short pause*) Seems like we're almost ready.

LUCA

Doesn't matter. I don't mind waiting.

MADELEINE H

I guess that's what you do in here?

LUCA

Yes, I guess . . . Do I look pale?

MADELEINE H

(*friendly*) Aaaah . . . no, I don't think so . . . but that wouldn't be so strange, would it? (*short pause*) This wasn't a very sunny fall.

LUCA

No, very bad weather, but it doesn't matter.

CAMERAMAN

I'm ready.

MADELEINE H

OK, thank you. (*She smiles towards Luca, the camera starts rolling, and then she turns to the camera.*) The fact that Imago, this time, is bringing up such a horrifying subject, a subject that, at first glance, doesn't seem to belong in a program such as this one, which mostly deals with art and cultural subjects, is because it has been noted as an example of how the borders between life and art have been erased; and it has also brought back to life the old discussion of how shocking events should be told, since there now are plans for making a film based on the murders. Does the artist have responsibility in choosing the subjects he wants to depict, and does he have any responsibility for how they affect and are received by the public? To briefly outline the actual tragedy . . . about a year ago both parents of Luca S. were found murdered in his apartment, and right away he became the prime suspect. He was arrested and immediately confessed to the crime. After the trial he was brought here, to the psychiatric crime unit clinic, where he is now waiting for the psychiatric evaluation to be completed, so that he'll finally receive a verdict. . . . His story clearly has elements, which bring to mind Greek tragedy. It has been described as a contemporary Oedipus drama, in so far as the participants did not, until the very last moment, understand the relationship they had to one another. Eric and Rosa Sabato, originally from Chile, were, due to their political activities during the sixties, forced to leave behind their young son, when they were expelled from their country, and they knew nothing of his fate. The son had been placed in a foster home. Twenty years later they were to reunite in Paris, a reunion that would result in catastrophic consequences. This last year we've also had no less than six productions of the old Greek tragedy playing here in Paris, in historical as well as contemporary interpretations. . . . We're wondering if that is a coincidence. Has the mask of civility been torn from us humans, due to the horribly cruel acts of violence that are surrounding us—the former Yugoslavia, the conflicts in the Middle East, the wars in Africa, the violence in our modern cities? Are we trapped in a social nightmare? Will we be exposed to even more examples of these Greek tragedies? . . . Haven't we, as humans, come any further than this? . . . Will generation after generation have to repeat the same disastrous tragedy, and is it the duty of the artist to try to explain unexplainable actions? (*turns to Luca*) Luca . . . were you, yourself, struck by the parallels to the famous Greek drama?

LUCA

(*smiling, aware of his good looks and position*) Yes, of course. Certainly. Without a question. On many different levels. Except that I didn't, like Oedipus, blind myself. I wanted to experience my fate and see my victims. . . . I mean, on a different level all of South America is one big example of a colossal Oedipus tragedy, where the corpses of fathers are stacked one on top of each other. . . . In the name of social revolutions, sons and fathers murder each other over and over again, but on such a grand scale that it loses all individual significance. Those are collective Oedipus tragedies. (*quick pause, smiles*) But, I mean, for me, that has not been of any comfort. Not until I knew, did I . . . even my foot . . . Oedipus also had a bum foot.

MADELEINE H

Which one of the murders do you think is the most . . . serious? Which one upsets you the most, the murder of your father or your mother?

LUCA

(*after a short pause*) Well . . . that was an unexpected question. . . . I've been asked about everything else. . . . I haven't thought about it . . . I don't know. . . . Now, I can't really separate them. . . . I knew my father a little better, but . . . murdering your mother might be a more serious crime. . . . It is in here in prison, anyway.

MADELEINE H

Can you tell us a little about your emotions concerning what has happened?

LUCA

No. (*pause*) I don't know what kind of emotions one would have.

MADELEINE H

But . . .

LUCA

Are you talking about remorse or something? . . . Well, it's hard to describe. I just look at it like the end of something, like the end of a chain
of circumstances that I couldn't influence in any way, that I couldn't stop
. . . as if there was no other option . . . as if I pushed myself into my life's
destiny.

MADELEINE H

How?

LUCA

But maybe all murders are . . . or look like . . . I don't know. (*short
pause*) It's difficult to explain. There were so many things that were going on at the same time. I didn't know them. . . . Well, Eric, my dad—I
still have a hard time calling him "Dad"—him I knew better, as I said,
but Rosa I had only met twice before it happened.

MADELEINE H

How come? . . . Why was she there? Why was she in your apartment?

LUCA

She came looking for me. She showed up. I didn't expect her. She just
showed up. She had followed me. . . . It was so silly. . . . If she hadn't
showed up, nothing would have happened. I had met her in a bookshop a
week before. Just a coincidence . . . and then she showed up at my place.

MADELEINE H

And what happened then?

LUCA

I told you already.

MADELEINE H

What happened then?

LUCA

She was very nice. (*short pause*) Not in any way a Greek . . . not some Greek Goddess.

MADELEINE H

Just an ordinary, unhappy woman.

LUCA

Yes, that's right. . . . Not in the beginning, but later . . . when she said I was her son, but then Eric was already there, because he came later.

MADELEINE H

Did she say that she was your mother?

LUCA

Yes, that's right. (*short pause*) I got very upset of course, and . . .

MADELEINE H

Did you believe her, that she was your mother?

LUCA

Yes, right away. I don't know why, but I believed her. I believed her. . . . As soon as I understood . . . and then when Eric . . . my father . . . came, and had his own key . . . then of course . . . then it became clear . . . but she probably knew already . . .

MADELEINE H

What became clear?

LUCA

Well . . . about the relationship.

MADELEINE H

(*after a pause*) The relationship between you and your father? Your physical relationship?

LUCA

Yes. (*short pause*) Yes.

MADELEINE H

You had a physical relationship?

LUCA

Yes. (*short pause*) Sure.

MADELEINE H

A love affair?

LUCA

Yes . . . I've had to talk about it so much with the psychologists, but I haven't . . . (*pause*) Oedipus didn't have anything with his father, did he?

MADELEINE H

No . . . no, I don't think so. (*pause*) And then . . . what happened then?

LUCA

Well . . . we talked a little. And then I killed them.

MADELEINE H

Did you know then that they were your mother and father?

LUCA

Yes. (*short pause*) That's right . . . but that's not why I did it, I did it . . . I've thought about it . . . I've tried to . . . I've talked about them a lot . . . but it was because . . . it was to help them really.

MADELEINE H

Help?

LUCA

Yes. (*short pause*) So that they wouldn't . . . so that they wouldn't have to be part of what had happened. It was the way it was supposed to be, as if I couldn't do anything else. I couldn't say, "OK, bye then, we won't see each other again." I wouldn't have been able to continue to live as usual either; but I did it mostly for their sake. . . . She was the first one. That was hard, because she didn't die right away. . . . So then again the knife cut across her neck. And then it was over. (*short pause*) That's when I, for the first time, understood the saying "from ear to ear." (*He has an impulse to laugh, but refrains himself.*) Then it was his turn. He wasn't supposed to see it, the way she looked. . . . That wasn't my intention. It was supposed to happen very quickly, so that he wouldn't have to see it. . . . Then he died too. (*short pause*) And then afterwards I was very tired. I felt like I'd been driving a car for days without any rest. I was extremely tired, completely pooped. I collapsed, then I fell asleep. I slept until the next day, to the middle of the day, and when I woke up I was hungry, and I went out to get something to eat. . . . And then I walked around for days on end all over the place. I don't know where I was or what I was doing. I didn't want to go back and see them. I knew what I had done, but I couldn't think about it, I didn't think about it. It was like it had been a dream, like it had been someone else.

MADELEINE H

And now? (*short pause*) What would you say to them if you met them today?

LUCA

Today? (*pause*) I don't know . . . I don't know. . . . What would I say?

MADELEINE H

Do you think they would forgive you?

LUCA

No. . . . I don't know. (*pause*) If anyone would, I guess it should be them . . . but . . . I don't know.

MADELEINE H

(*after a long pause*) Thank you. (*She pauses briefly, turns to the camera-man, nods, and he nods back.*)

LUCA

(*breaks the silence*) Was it all right? Was it OK?

MADELEINE H

Yes, I think so. . . . I think it's all right. (*short pause*) Do you know when they'll start shooting the film?

LUCA

In May, I think. . . . But they want to make some changes in the meeting between me and Rosa. Have it take place in a café. . . . Supposedly she sees me coming on some old, big motorcycle wearing a dark suit, a tuxedo shirt, and stuff like that. I'm supposed to have worked in some restaurant, and then she would come out and there would be something going on between me and her. . . . But the night I met her I had been at the hospital and been part of a post-mortem . . . and then afterwards I was supposed to be driving around Paris on my motorcycle. But I've told them to tell it like it was. I'd like it to be the way it was. I don't want them to change anything.

THE END

WAR

Characters

A, The mother

B, Beenina, daughter, 15-16 years old

C, Semira, daughter, 12-13 years old

D, The father

E, Uncle Ivan

The action takes place somewhere in Eastern Europe.

1.

A shabby yard. A damaged stone wall containing a door frame. A wooden table. A couple of plastic chairs. Harsh lighting. A couple of old cardboard boxes. Two mattresses on the floor.

A

(*is straightening up the house*) Go wash up, Semira. Wash up.

C

But the water is so filthy. (*goes over to get some bread*)

A

No, first you have to wash up.

C

The water is dirty.

A

Wash yourself well . . . and get dressed . . . go and get dressed.

(*B helps C to get dressed. C starts to sing.*)

C

Hurry up. I'm cold. (*C tickles her back.*)

B

Stop it . . . stop it.

A

You've gotten so big, both of you. (*She makes the bed.*) Come over here and help me. . . . Come here. (*grabs hold of her right arm*)

C

Wrong arm!

A

Sorry.

C

Couldn't we buy some new sheets? They are so dirty. They're shitty and full of green peas and piss. They stink.

A

You stink, you're the one who stinks.

C

What did I look like when I was born?

B

You were just an itty bitty piece of shit.

A

You were disgusting.

C

No . . . and how big was I?

(*A bends down to show with her hand that C was tiny.*)

C

That's not true. And Beenina, what about her?

B

I was bigger, I've always been bigger than you.

C

What would my name have been if I was a boy?

B

Semiro, Semiro, the ass of a cow!

C

Beenina, Beenina, hair on the arms! I'd like to have a little brother or a little sister who I could torture.

A

What did you say?

C

For Christmas, I really want a little brother for Christmas.

A

Fine, write a letter to Santa, "Dear Santa, I'd like to . . ."

C

Couldn't we get a little brother when Daddy comes back? I'm sure Daddy would like to . . . (*silence*)

B

And you? Would you want that?

C

Did you already live here?

A

Yes, of course. You're so silly.

C

Where did I sleep?

A

(*points to a cardboard box*) There.

B

What about me? Where did I sleep?

A

In the other one. (*pause*) Stop it now, it's enough.

(*C wraps herself up in a sheet; A takes it away from her; C runs towards B.*)

B

(*picks up a cassette, plays it, screams*) They're incredible! They're so fucking awesome! I'll play them at my funeral.

C

When?

B

When I'm dead. Because they're so fucking great! (*turns it off*)

C

No.

B

It's over.

C

I want to hear more.

B

I don't have time.

C

Can't we hear one more? Just one more?

B

No. Shut up. (*sits down*)

C

What are you going to wear at your funeral? Are you going to wear your red skirt?

B

(*starts to put on lipstick*) Nothing.

C

You're not wearing anything? Are you going to be naked?

B

Yes, completely naked.

C

Why? . . . I'm going to wear a white dress and white, silk shoes. The whole dress is going to be covered with glitter, or those tiny mirrors that shine. And then under it I'll wear a teddy. (*laughs*) I'll be lying down with my hands in prayer. . . . What about your head? Are you going to wear a hat?

B

(*makes her lips into a kiss*) Where's the mirror?

C

You've put too much on.

B

It has to show.

C

Well, it does. A lot.

B

It has to show in the dark.

C

You don't look like yourself.

B

I'm not.

C

What? (*silence*). What if Daddy saw you now?

B

Which Daddy?

C

There's only one Daddy. . . . He'd be so sad.

                                    B
He's dead so it doesn't matter.

                                    C
How do you know?

                                    B
What?

                                    C
That he's dead. Maybe he's alive.

                                    B
Of course he isn't.

                                    C
But maybe he'll be coming home again.

                                    B
Then he would have been home a long time ago.

                                    C
I think he's coming back . . . and that he's young.

                                    B
Young?

                                    C
Yes, like he was before the war.

                                    B
Tell her he's dead?

                                    A
What did you say?

B

Daddy. Tell her that he's dead. (*pause)* Dead. (*pause*) Stone dead. (*silence*). He's dead, isn't he?

A

I don't know.

B

Daddy. Of course he's dead.

A

Who knows?

B

Yes, but that's what you think.

A

Yes, what should I think?

C

He isn't dead until he doesn't come back any more.

B

You idiot, he hasn't come back, has he?

C

Yes, but he could, maybe . . . we could try to act as if he was alive anyway. We don't have to act like . . . I mean just because he isn't here right now.

B

Maybe he's living in Italy renting out beach chairs to fat tourists.

C

I hope he comes home again . . . before I get big, and gives me a smack.

B

Maybe he has a new young wife and two new kids and a new dog.

C

Shut up . . . I'll cut your tits off.

B

(*picks up the jawbone of an animal*) You've lost your teeth.

A

Could you go and get the water?

B

I already got it this morning. It's her turn.

C

I don't want to.

B

Why?

C

Because I don't want to.

B

It's not dangerous.

A

Go with her, or half will spill out.

B

I brought two pails in this morning.

C

I'm afraid.

A

Then I will go.

B

You're the mother, after all. (*silence*) If they want to do something they'll just walk in. (*to C*) They like silly, little brats like you, because you don't have any infectious diseases yet.

A

Stop it.

C

Woof, woof, woof, woof. (*throws the animal head*) That's just Dino.

B

But it's true.

A

Don't talk like that.

B

They don't care. They rape you and then they piss in your face. Your stupid face.

A

Remember that she's a child.

B

Child?

A

She's just a child.

B

There are no children any more. (*silence*)

A

Are you going to help me or not?

B

Isn't that what I'm doing? What am I doing if not . . .

A

Yeah . . .

B

If I'm not helping you, what am I doing then?

A

I'm sorry.

B

What am I doing?

A

I'm sorry . . . so sorry.

B

I could've taken off a long time ago and not given a shit about the two of you. I could've been living in Germany instead of doing this. I could've left with a lot of guys if I wanted to, if I was only thinking about myself.

A

Sure.

C

You can't even speak German.

B

So what? I could still manage. I know the words I need to know.

A

What would you do in Germany?

B

What am I doing here? (*short pause*) Yesterday there was someone who asked me to go with him and live in his big house in Munich. He was some big boss for Mercedes. He had a TV in his car. We watched an American movie. And then we saw a film from the war. Lots of skinny guys walking around in a prison camp. Maybe daddy is one of them, but who knows, they all look the same. (*silence*)

C

Are you going to do it?

B

What?

C

Go to Germany? Are you going to Germany?

B

Maybe.

C

Can I have your blanket then?

(*D enters, they don't notice him. He stops a few steps from the gate and waits. C notices him. She gets very frightened and runs over to A, who is standing behind her in her shadow. Then B notices him, stands up slowly, and unconsciously wipes off some of the lipstick on her lips. C is pulling at her mother's sleeve.*)

A

Why don't you call me mommy any longer? (*pause*) If someone really wanted me I would . . . (*A looks at B and then notices what B is looking at. No one moves.*) No. (*silence*)

D

It's me.

A

No.

D

I've come home.

A

No. . . . (*silence*)

D

What are you doing?

A

What do you want?

D

Did everyone . . .

A

Good God . . . (*silence*) I didn't think that . . .

D

What?

A

No?

D

That I would come back?

A

What are you wearing? Are those shoes? (*silence*)

(*D walks very slowly into the backyard. He's wearing a long, worn out military coat and is trying to find his bearings.*)

D

Give me a chair. Isn't there a chair I could sit on? (*A brings one of the chairs and puts it in front of him. D tries to find it and then sits down.*) I need to sit. I've been walking for a very long time. I've walked very far. (*silence*) How are things? (*silence*) Where are the girls?

A

They are . . .

D

Are they alive?

A

They're here.

D

Where? Where are they? (*silence*) It's been a while . . . it's been a while since I was home.

A

Yes.

D

I guess about two years.

A

I thought . . . I didn't think I would see you again alive . . . and then you're standing there, without a word . . . without saying anything.

D

What's there to say?

A

I was sure you'd never come back again.

D

But I did. (*silence*) Where are they . . . Semira and Beenina?

A

They're standing right there . . .

D

Yes. . . . (*pause*) It takes a while. . . . Tell them to come here. Tell them to come and say hello to their father. Tell them he's home again. Tell them he's alive and that he's come home.

A

They can see that you are here. (*They are silent, then she pushes C.*) Go
to him.

C

No.

A

You don't have to be afraid.

C

I'm not afraid.

A

We weren't sure who it was.

C

I saw who it was.

D

(*holding his arms out*) Come here and say hello.

B

(*She walks slowly up to him and puts her hand out.*) Hello.

D

Hello. (*He feels her hand, stands up, and hugs her.*) Semira?

B

No, it's Beenina.

D

Is that you, my little girl?

B

Yes.

D

My little girl. (*B tries to get out of his embrace. He touches her face, gets lipstick on his hands, and smells it.*) What's this?

B

Nothing.

D

What's this on your face?

B

It's nothing.

D

What have you done?

B

Just vaseline.

C

It's lipstick.

D

Go and wash it off.

C

Someone gave it to her.

B

No, that's not true. It's mine.

D

You aren't a whore, are you?

A

It's just lipstick. All girls wear it.

D

Not my girls. Only whores wear that. Go and wash your face.

A

It doesn't mean anything.

D

My children shouldn't look like whores.

C

I'm not wearing any.

A

You two are supposed to go and bring back some water. (*pause*) I guess you're hungry. (*silence*)

D

What the hell have you been doing while I was gone?

A

We have tried to survive.

D

Yes, I noticed. (*silence*)

A

What's wrong with your eyes?

D

My eyes?

A

You don't look at us.

D

The most important thing is I'm home.

A

You don't look at me when you speak. . . .You keep turning your face away.

D

Well, that's what you're supposed to do. . . . It says so in the Holy Book. (*pause*) Maybe I'm looking for something else.

A

What are you saying?

D

I'm not saying anything. (*silence*)

A

Can't you see?

D

Some shit got into my eyes.

A

Are you blind?

D

I manage.

A

What are we to do then?

D

Maybe I'll be able to see again one of these days, with the help of God.

A

How did you find your way back here?

D

Maybe you didn't want me to.

                              A

Did someone help you?

                              D

Who would help me? Who would want to help me?

                              A

Are you blind, you idiot?

                              D

(*after a long pause*) Aren't you grateful that I'm alive?

                              A

Grateful? (*pause*) What do I have to be grateful for? (*silence*)

(*C looks at A, then at D, then at A again, who's standing perfectly still. Then she carefully goes up to D, who senses that someone is close to him. He brings up his hand, it hits C, and she screams out.*)

                              D

Who is this?

                              C

It's just me.

                              D

Semira?

                              C

It's me. I just wanted to hug you.

                              D

You've got to be careful. . . . How was I to know who it was?

                              C

I just wanted to . . .

D

It's fine. Come here to me. (*C walks up to him.*) I didn't know who it was. (*reaches out with his right hand*) Now everything is fine. *(touches her face)* Nothing to worry about. *(feels her face, her lips*) You aren't wearing any shit on your face, are you?

C

No . . . I'm too young.

D

That's good. . . . Smile.

C

Yes.

D

Be happy.

C

Yes.

D

Are you happy?

C

I don't know. No, only the stupid ones are happy.

D

So, how old are you now?

C

Thirteen . . . soon.

B

You're just twelve?

C

Yes, but I'll be thirteen soon.

D

Yes, in May.

C

May seventh.

D

May is good . . . it's a good month. (*He lifts her up and puts her on his knee.*) Wow, you got so heavy. Did you have a lot to eat for breakfast?

C

No. I only eat the food God gives us.

D

It's very fashionable to be thin these days.

C

Yes. (*silence*) Will you never ever see again?

D

Only God can answer that.

C

Why?

D

Because that's how it is.

C

So then you can't see me?

D

Yes . . . I can see you.

C

How?

D

I see you . . . just as well as if I could see.

C

You do?

B

He remembers what you looked like before.

C

Because I'm so pretty.

B

You?

A

Go get the water and find some wood so that we can get some food going.

C

Are you eating with us?

B

Why shouldn't he?

D

Maybe there's not enough food?

A

Just go.

C

I don't want to. I want to be with my daddy.

D

Go ahead. . . . You'll be with me later, now that I'm home.

C

Is Uncle Ivan . . .

(*A throws a pitcher on the ground. D dives down onto the dirt.*)

A

What the hell? . . . Go! How many times do I have to tell you before you
do what I say?

B

Quit your fucking nagging, bitch.

C

Come on.

B

Let her get it herself.

(*C takes B's hand, they exit*)

D

What was that? I thought it was . . .

A

I dropped a pitcher. Now there are broken pieces everywhere, so you
better watch out.

D

(*stands up*) You should be more careful. (*lights a cigarette*) You got to
take care of what you have, however little it is. (*A picks up the broken
pieces.*) How are things? (*pause*) Did you miss me?

A

Did you see a doctor about your eyes?

D

How could I? (*short pause*) Don't you understand anything?

A

I was just asking.

D

Do you think there were any doctors there?

A

What are you going to do?

D

Where do you think I've been? On vacation? I've been in a place where people ate shit. It wasn't a vacation.

A

No . . .

D

Seems to me that's what you think. (*lights a cigarette*) Tell me . . .

A

What?

D

How . . . how are you?

A

What do you think?

D

Well, I guess it's a little better now that it's warmer.

A

What's there to tell?

D

One can spend time outdoors anyway. (*pause*) How's the house?

A

You know. (*silence*)

D

Have you had enough food?

A

Otherwise we'd be dead. . . . We got some chickens from our neighbor when they moved into the city.

D

To their cousin? Yes, he lives in the city. He's lived there for years.

A

They left in March.

D

In March?

A

Yes. They got old. But they're alive.

D

That's because they're old.

A

Toni is dead.

D

There are so many dead. (*silence*)

A

Look how thin you are.

D

The last months we only ate what we found on the ground. We worked in a factory where they made tractors. We chewed on pieces of asphalt we found on the ground. I thought I would come home and get fattened up. (*silence*) Where are you?

A

Here.

D

What are you doing?

A

I'm standing here.

D

Really. (*short pause*) Why are you so far away?

A

I'm here.

D

Really. (*short pause*) How's the roof? Does it leak?

A

Only when it's raining. Then the water comes in all over the place.

D

That's what I meant.

A

It leaks in the kitchen and the bedroom.

D

That's what I meant.

A

But now it hasn't rained for two months.

D

Then it must be dry.

A

Yes. (*short pause*) We have no lights . . . but they say it will come back in a couple of weeks.

D

They say so many things. So many things. (*There is silence. A turns her head.*) Are you still there?

A

Yes.

D

I had this feeling that you left.

A

No, I'm still here.

D

I thought you moved away.

A

No.

D

We'll have to get the roof repaired. (*short pause*) We have to . . . one way or another.

A

There's no hurry. . . . They used the mosque as a parking garage.

D

Parking garage?

A

They parked their cars and motorcycles there.

D

I'm sure they did.

C

(*comes back*) Daddy, Daddy, Daddy . . . I've picked some flowers for you. One pink and three white ones. They smell good. They're plastic.

D

Thank you.

C

We brought the water.

D

Good. Give me a glass of water. (*C brings him the water.*) Thank you.

A

Just think if you can never see again. (*short pause*) How will you manage?

C

I can help Daddy.

D

(*after a while*) I guess I'm still the same?

C

I can help you. (*silence*) Soon I can do everything.

D

Yes.

C

I can take care of you until I get big.

D

Yes. (*pause*) How's Sharif?

A

Sharif?

D

Yes. Where's he?

A

Gone.

D

Gone?

A

Like the others.

D

And Ismael?

A

He too. . . . It's almost a year ago.

D

Yes, of course.

A

They came and took all the men one night. They had no time to hide. Since then we haven't seen them.

D

Where are they?

A

Only the ones who took them know.

D

Well, they'll probably turn up one of these days.

A

They say they're buried on the other side of the Black Valley.

D

Then they're close to home, anyway.

A

No one dares to go there. (*silence*)

D

And Ivan?

A

Ivan?

D

Yes. (*silence*). Aren't you going to tell me about him?

A

Well . . . he . . . he . . . (*looks at B and C*)

D

He's probably hiding somewhere.

A

Why?

D

That's what he always did when things got tough.

A

No, he . . . I don't know. I haven't seen him . . . since before the new year.

D

Well, at least they don't have to think about what happened to them. (*short pause*) The dead ones don't have to remember how they died. We are the ones who are forced to remember.

A

It was in the evening. (*short pause*) Just as they were being taken away it began to snow, and after a while you couldn't see their footprints. (*silence*)

D

How come you all made it? Why aren't you dead? (*silence*) Answer me.

A

Why?

D

Why? Why are you alive?

A

Well . . . ask God.

D

God?

A

Don't ask me. Ask Him.

D

I'm asking you.

A

Ask Him.

D

I'm asking you.

A

What should I say? (*short pause*) I'd rather be dead. (*silence*) But I'm not.

D

What? (*short pause*) Don't tell me. I don't want to know.

A

I wouldn't tell you anyway.

D

What I don't know I don't know. I need to rest. I want to feel like I'm home.

(*darkness*)

2.

(*light*)

D

(*lies down on the mattress*) Who is it?

A

It's me.

D

I want to be alone.

A

I'll leave you alone. I was just getting my sweater.

D

Wait. (*short pause*) Come here.

A

It's getting cold.

D

Come here and . . .

A

I'm cooking.

D

Stay here . . . talk to me.

A

About what?

D

I guess there's a lot we have to talk about. (*short pause*) Where are you?

A

Here . . .

D

What are you doing?

A

Getting dressed . . .

D

In what?

A

Pants . . . I told you it's getting cold.

D

I don't know what's wrong with you. (*short pause*) Are you looking at me?

A

No.

D

Come closer and look at me. (*short pause*) Are you looking at me?

A

Yes . . . it's dark, it's hard to see.

D

I want to feel you're looking at me. Then it doesn't feel so lonely. (*silence*) Sometimes I have the feeling that all I have to do is to reach out and turn on a light and I'll be able to see again . . . clearly and sharply. Maybe it would have been easier, this darkness, if I hadn't once had eyes to see with and knew how everything looked. It's as if the world had died. I'm walking around thinking everything is like it was, but it's not.

Maybe there isn't that much to see. Maybe one should, when everything is said and done, be grateful that one can't see. Since it was better before. (*He takes out a pack of cigarettes from his pocket and lights a cigarette.*) Well, there's nothing to be done. In the camp we snatched the Holy Book from someone and pulled out the pages and used them to roll cigarettes. The paper was so fine, so thin. (*hands her the cigarette*) Do you want one?

A

No. I've got to go now.

D

Come here.

A

I've too much to do. (*silence*)

D

Come here.

A

No, what do you want?

D

Come here, I said. (*silence*)

A

What do you want?

D

What do I want? I want you to behave like the woman I took as my wife. That's what I want. That's all I want.

A

It's not the way it was.

D

What the hell do you mean by that?

A

So much has happened . . . while you were gone.

D

I don't give a damn. I'm your husband. I have my rights. I want what's
mine.

A

It's not how it was. . . . I'm not the way I was.

D

I'm not either . . . But we can be, if we want to.

A

Like I was? . . . The person I was? The one you left?

D

Stop talking.

A

Don't you understand? (*short pause*) I thought you were dead.

D

I was. (*silence*) Where are you? (*short pause*) I can't see you. (*silence*)
Are you still here?

A

Yes.

D

What the hell, answer me then. (*walks towards her*)

A

Am I supposed to make noise the whole time so you'll know where I am?

D

Stay there. (*He walks towards her.*) Say something. (*silence*) Stay still.
(*silence*)

A

I'm leaving now.

D

Stay still, you goddam cunt. (*A stops in the middle of the room and then leaves.*) You are mine whether I see you or not. (*walks around, turns around, stops*) Do you hear me? (*C quietly comes into the room. D hears a sound. There is silence.*) I know you're there . . . I hear your breathing. (*C has a long stick and lightly pokes his stomach.*) What are you doing? (*C pokes him a few times, going for his eyes.*) What the hell, don't do that. (*He hits the air, walks around in the room, then sits down.*)

C

(*pretends she is coming into the room.*) Daddy?

D

Who is it?

C

It's me.

D

Get lost.

C

We're eating now.

D

Get lost, I said.

C

What are you doing?

D

Go away.

C

I'm just getting my book.

                              D

Get it and get lost.

                              C

Can I help you with something?

                              D

What the hell could you do to help me? (*silence*) What are you doing?

                              C

I'm walking back and forth. I'm just walking back and forth swinging
my skirt, trying to make myself happy. But it isn't easy . . . the way the
world looks today.

                              D

Come here.

                              C

(*walks up to him*) What do you want?

                              D

Come here. (*embraces her, lifts her up, holds her.*)

                              C

Not so hard.

                              D

No, not so hard. (*silence*)

                              C

You don't smell like you did before. You smell like something else.

                              D

I smell like hunger, like starvation.

                              C

I'm reading a book about a girl who's my age. She wrote it herself. She
had to hide with her mom and dad in a secret room in the attic, because

she was different and the Germans wanted to kill all of them during the
war. I got it from Uncle Ivan last year on my birthday. He reads a lot. It
was his book. You can't buy it in a store any more. It's the only book I
have left. They burned the other books, but I had hidden this one in a
place where they couldn't find it. I've read it seven times. But it doesn't
matter. I could read it over and over again. I think she was killed later.
Soon I'll be older than her. Mommy and Beenina said that you were
dead. But I knew you were alive. I knew that you would come back
home again. (*silence*) Are we going to move away?

D

Who said that?

C

Mommy. She says that we are moving to a different country where
there's food and clothes and where I can go to school.

D

We aren't moving anywhere.

C

No, I don't want to move. It doesn't matter that much that you can't see.
It's sad for you, but it would probably be worse if you couldn't walk.
There's a boy in my class who doesn't have any arms any more. And
then there's one with only one leg. But he plays soccer anyway. He
wants to be a soccer star. They play soccer all the time. But since we
don't go to school right now it doesn't matter. Mommy said that I was
going to the hospital because I was so scared. I was shaking all the time.
I couldn't eat or sleep. But now I'm not scared. Now we'll kill all of
them, and then they can't do anything to us anymore. Then everything
will be fine. I'll go to school and when I come home I'll read the paper to
you, and I can get things for you. Beenina wants to go away, but I don't
know where she'd go. She's saving money to do it, but I'm going to stay
and take care of you and Mommy. Maybe she'll visit after she's been
gone for a while. Then she'll bring us super nice presents and take me to
Disneyland. She's promised she'd take me there before I'm eighteen.

(*darkness*)

3.

(light)

(All four are sitting outside eating. The light is strong.)

C

Is there more?

A

No, you know there isn't.

C

I'm still hungry.

A

You eat more than all of us.

B

She can have mine.

A

You haven't touched it.

B

I don't want anything. . . . It's too warm.

A

You have to eat. You can't survive on chewing-gum and coca cola.

B

I eat . . . I eat when I feel like it.

D

You can have mine. *(gives his bread to C)*

C

She gets food from them.

(*B hits C.*)

D

Them? Who are "them?"

A

The people she's helping. . . . They give her food sometimes.

D

Who are they?

A

Those who are helping us.

C

The people who won. . . . They are the ones helping us now.

D

What do they help us with?

C

I don't know.

D

They burned our villages and towns, they put our children on fire so that they burned like torches. . . . Are those the ones helping us?

C

They have air conditioning and refrigerators. (*silence*)

D

What's going on with you?

A

Nothing.

C

No.

D

Well, but try to be a little cheerful then.

B

I'm full of cheer.

C

Me too.

D

So show it then.

B

We are as cheerful as larks.

C

Peep, peep, peep . . . (*silence*)

D

(*turns to A*) What about you? Are you happy I'm home? What else could you be? You could use a man, couldn't you? There are many men who don't give a fuck about coming home again. They get themselves new women and new children. Think about it. You should be grateful I'm not like that. (*In silence, D puts his hand out as if he was patting a dog.*)

A

(*She picks up the gum wrapper from B and looks at it.*) I haven't seen colors in so long.

D

Dino. Where is he?

A

Dino?

D

The dog. Where did he go?

A

He's lost.

D

How?

A

He died.

D

He died?

B

That was forever ago.

D

Did they kill him too? They couldn't even let a poor, innocent creature stay alive. (*silence*) What did they do to him?

A

Well, it . . .

B

Tell him the way it is. You never tell it like it is. You're always lying.

C

The truth sets us free. But some truths you should forget.

A

We had to kill him.

D

Why?

B

We were hungry.

A

We hadn't eaten for weeks. . . . We didn't know what to do.

C

We ate grass.

D

You ate him? You ate Dino?

A

What were we to do?

C

He was just a dog.

B

We pretended he was something else.

C

I pretended that it was chicken paprika.

D

Couldn't you have pretended he was something more elegant? Lamb chops, maybe?

B

There was no food for him either.

C

Mommy said he would've starved to death anyway.

B

They don't feel anything. They don't understand what's happening like we do, like people do.

C

No, but I was sad. Poor Dino.

B

You ate more than any of us; you even ate the tail.

C

So? He didn't need it anymore.

D

Well, anyway, he would've been happy that I came home.

C

They ate us too.

B

Who?

C

Yes, they ate people . . . the dogs did.

B

Yes, but they're dogs.

C

Sometimes I put out his bowl of water and call for him, and then I remember that I ate him. (*silence*)

B

Couldn't we go to another country?

C

Yeah, the country of Disney.

A

Who would want us?

D

Has anything else happened?

B

No.

D

What about going to school? Have you been going to school?

B

No.

C

Are you kidding?

D

Why not?

C

We weren't allowed.

B

They didn't want us to learn anything.

C

We're studying at home instead. Uncle Ivan is helping us when he has time . . . when he had time . . . a long time ago.

B

That was years ago.

C

That's what I said.

A

He just tried to help them with math and English a couple of times before he disappeared.

D

Yes, he always had the time for those things.

B

If you know English you'll get by anywhere.

D

Not where I was.

C

There are forty-two pages missing in my English book.

A

It's getting really cold.

D

Cold?

A

Yes.

D

No, it feels good. (*short pause*) Why did he help them? Why not you? Since you were a teacher. (*E enters the yard. He is about to say hello but notices D. A lifts her hand to warn him about saying anything. The girls look at E, then at D, then at A. A waves her hand to signal E to leave, but he stays.*) What is it?

A

What?

D

What's going on? (*waves his hand*)

B

It's the flies. She was waving away some flies. (*waves her hand*)

C

(*waves her hand*) Flies, flies, flies . . .

A

So many flies here.

D

I don't see any flies.

B

No, now they're gone.

C

There's one . . . on the bread.

D

It's too early for flies.

A

Yes, I guess it's the sun. (*tries to get E to leave, but he stays*)

C

They are so small. . . . They are the worst. They crawl into your eyes and mouth and other places.

A

Why don't we go inside?

D

No, I like it here. . . . It's nice to sit in the sun. . . . Well, I don't need any sunglasses, anyway. (*laughs*)

C

Every cloud has a silver lining.

D

You're right. (*silence*) Give me some water. (*B pours water into his cup. He drinks.*) This water, you can't go wrong with. There's no water on earth like it. . . . Wonder what kind of summer we'll have this year? Will it be as dry as it was three years ago?

(*E slowly walks up to them. He stops a couple of feet away from them.*)

C

There were so many dead bodies in the river,t we couldn't go swimming.

A

(*lifts her finger to her mouth*) That's true.

D

Of course it's true. That summer the river was already dried up in July. (*In silence he drinks more water.*) Yes, Ivan, he thought he would get somewhere. He was too good to work in the factory like the rest of us. He was going to be something better. An attorney or a doctor. Full of dreams and good-for-nothing. Not a plumber or a carpenter. Couldn't even drive a car. If you asked him to do something, he kept turning around and around like a dog looking for a place to shit. For him it was lucky that we had a war.

C

(*to Ivan*) That's my daddy.

A

Let's go inside.

D

Why?

A

You can stay.

C

Yes, stay here.

D

Yes. We'll sit here in the sun until evening. Then we'll go inside and lock the door. (*E is standing behind B, straight across from D. D reaches out for A's hand and takes it.*) Everything will be fine. We have to get used to it. Soon we'll think everything is back to normal again. You'll forget that I had eyes once upon a time. Human beings can get used to everything . . . as long as they have a little time to adjust. I still am who I am. I'm no one else. (*short pause*) When we were in the prison camp we used to talk about what it would be like when the war was over and we would be free again. . . . And everyone wanted it to be just like it was before . . . that everything would be like usual . . .

(*darkness*)

4.

(*light*)

(*Outside, in the dusk, E and A are standing across from each other.*)

E

So, he's back.

A

Yes, he got here this afternoon. He just stood there by the gate.

E

How nice.

A

I thought I saw a ghost. (*silence*)

E

So he made it.

A

It was awful. (*silence*)

E

Why was he talking about me as if I was dead?

A

Because I had to . . .

E

What?

A

. . . tell him you were dead.

E

That I'm dead?

A

Yes, what else could I say? (*short pause*) I didn't know what to say.

E

I see.

A

He's blind. He can't see any more.

E

I guess that's lucky . . . in a way.

A

I had to come up with something. I got so scared. I thought it was a ghost that came to . . .

E

Yes, sure. (*silence*) At first I didn't understand why he didn't react . . . and then I realized he couldn't see me.

A

Just think if you'd said something.

E

It was close. . . . I was about to go up to him and give him a hug. . . . I don't know what made me stop.

A

What are we going to do?

E

Yeah, that's the question.

A

What are we going to do now?

E

I don't know. (*silence*) So, he made it back anyway, huh? . . . They didn't manage to kill him. Well, some of them had to make it.

A

He thinks everything will be like before.

E

Like before?

A

Yes, that's what he wants.

E

Well of course, why wouldn't he? (*silence*) And you told him I was dead?

A

No, not exactly, but . . .

E

But maybe that's what you want . . .

A

He thinks you're dead.

E

What did he say about it?

A

He didn't say very much.

E

Did he say anything?

A

No.

E

Did he ask how I died?

A

I just said that you disappeared . . . some time before the new year, when it was snowing.

E

What are we going to do now?

A

I don't know.

E

He's my brother.

A

I know. (*silence*)

E

And where am I supposed to sleep tonight?

A

I don't know . . .

E

Are you going to sleep in the same bed?

A

I don't know . . . I want to be with you.

E

Are you two going to sleep together?

A

No. I don't know him. It's like he's a stranger. I love you.

E

But this is his house.

A

I love you. (*silence*)

E

Maybe it's better to tell.

A

What?

E

How things are. Between you and me.

A

No.

E

Better that he hears it from you than from others.

A

(*quietly*) Better if he was dead.

E

He has to know sooner or later.

A

I don't know what I'm saying. . . . I don't mean what I'm saying. (*silence*)

E

We aren't to blame. It's the war.

A

Yes, it's the war.

E

But I can't be walking around here pretending I don't exist.

A

No.

E

No . . . you've got to talk to him tomorrow.

A

I'll tell him I love you. (*silence*) If only he wasn't your brother . . .

E

I was sure he was dead.

A

Me too.

E

I can't help it if he's my brother. I didn't choose him. (*silence*) What are we going to do?

A

I don't know.

E

Do you want me to leave?

A

No.

E

Maybe that would be the best . . . for all of us.

A

No, you can't.

E

Maybe I should anyway.

A

No, you can't leave me.

E

I could find a way to get to Germany. There's work there. I could make some money.

A

You can't leave me.

E

Start over, find a better life, forget this shit. I'm not afraid to start over, not at all. There's nothing here anyway. Only graves. You have a husband.

A

You are my husband. He and I never had what we have together.

E

That's easy to say.

A

It's true.

E

Yes, maybe it's true. A dog that changes its owners also thinks it's true.

A

I was dead when I was with him. It didn't matter what happened to me. I couldn't feel anything. I couldn't speak. But when you came I started to live again, for the first time. I've never been as happy as I've been this last year, in spite of war, hunger, dirt, fear. I'm grateful for the war. . . . But I knew it. (*pause*) I knew it already the first time.

E

What did you know?

A

I knew you wouldn't stay . . . that one day you would leave me.

E

Well, I haven't left you yet.

A

You will though. . . . What do you want with an old woman with two grown children? I'm not even beautiful, just a skeleton. I have nothing.

E

I wasn't leaving . . . but now that he's back . . .

A

Maybe somewhere there's . . . maybe there is a home where . . . for the blind.

E

There aren't even homes for those of us who can see. (*He walks up to the window and looks in.*) There, he's sitting . . . staring . . .

A

What are we to do? (*short pause*) What are we going to do tonight?

(*darkness*)

5.

(*light*)

(*B comes home. C notices B, runs up to her, and follows her.*)

C

How was work today?

(*B sits down on the mattress. C makes a somersault and sits down next to B, who is counting her bills in her purse. C reaches out to grab the money. B pushes her away. C tries to tickle B.*)

B

Stop it. . . . Come on . . . (*tickles C*)

C

Stop . . . stop . . . I'm peeing.

B

I know, we sleep in the same bed.

C

(*hits her with her pillow*) Smells like Dino.

B

Look. (*shows her the bills*) There were three of them.

C

Three at the same time?

B

They were Americans . . .

C

Was it disgusting? What did they do? . . . Did you get ice cream? (*silence*)

B

Where do you think you are? Disneyland? (*pause*) One of them came from Wyoming-ing-ing-ding. He is going to become a priest.

C

The priest from Wyoming.

B

They're still better than the Russians.

C

I know.

B

They treated me like a whore. (*She's breathing in some glue from a plastic bag. C tries to get the bag. B looks at her and holds the bag in front of her face.*) Breathe in . . . breathe in. . . . Hard . . . hard, hard, hard . . .

C

(*is coughing.*) It stings. It itches. . . . I'm high.

(*They lie down on the mattress.*)

B

(*singing, louder and louder.*) In a little opening in a little forest a soldier is fucking a beautiful girl. There's blood everywhere. The soldier was the first. . . . (*C also sings. B hugs C.*) Je t'aime. You're so young, you don't understand anything. (*A comes in, pulls at B and pulls her away.*) No.

(*darkness*)

6.

(*light*)

(*C and D are lying on the mattress. A comes in.*)

D

Where have you been?

A

I was just outside.

D

At this hour? Why? (*silence*) What?

A

What?

D

What were you doing out there?

A

Nothing.

D

Did you just sit out there? (*silence*) Is it calm?

A

Calm?

D

Yes, the weather?

A

It's dark.

D

Of course it's dark, it's night. . . . The first night in my house. I guess there aren't any lights out there anymore. (*pause*) In the other houses. No lights out there any longer.

A

There aren't any houses left.

D

That's what I mean. . . . I guess there aren't many people left either. (*silence*) Are there many stars?

A

Stars?

D

In the sky.

A

Yes, I guess. (*short pause*) Aren't you going to sleep?

D

Why should I? (*silence, sits up*) I'm not stupid just because I can't see any longer. I'll manage. I'm still young, thirty-eight. My grandfather made it to ninety-three and drove vegetables into town until he was ninety. I have a lot left in me. As long as I gain some weight I'll . . . things can happen . . . I can learn. . . . There must be things a blind person can do. (*silence*) Aren't you coming to bed?

A

Yeah, soon.

D

They took it quite well. . . . They'll get used to it.

A

The girls?

D

Yes, they took it well.

A

What else could they do?

D

They were just kids when I left. . . . Now they're big . . . both our girls.

A

Yes, our girls, they're big.

D

But they'll always look to me like they did that day I last saw them. (*short pause*) That's what's kept me going . . . that's what I've been thinking about day and night . . . the hope that I would be coming back to see them again.

A

They were so happy. (*silence*)

D

I'm grateful my parents died, so that they didn't have to see me like this.
. . . Lucky for them that they died before their children did. (*short pause*)
Every night we kept digging graves, because we knew that we would use
them for someone the next day. . . . One morning it was my father and
my mother that I was washing and . . . where are you?

A

I didn't do anything.

D

What?

A

I'm mending a skirt. (*She is sitting, holding the brother's pants in her
lap, absolutely still.*)

D

I was just wondering what you were doing.

A

I'm mending . . . whatever can be repaired.

D

(*short pause*) The worst thing for them would've been if they had to bury
Ivan. He was their favorite.

A

Yes. . . . Was he?

D

Yes, he was their bright light. The beloved son. . . . I guess because he
came last. He was the one who would become something big. They sold
a piece of land just to pay for his studies at the university. They were
hoping that he would become a medical doctor . . . a doctor because there

will always be a need for doctors. Doctors and shoemakers. (*short pause*)
He even wrote poetry. . . . That he had time for. He wasn't even there for
their funeral. (*silence*) How did he die?

A

Who?

D

Ivan, my brother.

A

I don't know. Like the others.

D

You can tell me. There's still nothing that could be worse than what I've
experienced.

A

I don't know anything. I only know that he disappeared.

D

Last year?

A

Yes.

D

Maybe he isn't even dead.

A

Yeah.

D

Who knows? Maybe he'll show up one of these days. I came back even
if no one had counted on it. Least of all myself.

A

Right.

D

You never know. . . . I was accompanied from the train station by someone who had been in the same prison camp as me, but in a different building. He got hold of a boy down by the station and asked him to run ahead to his parents and tell them that he was alive and that they shouldn't get frightened when they saw him, because he was looking so thin and sick. But even though they had been warned, his mother fainted when she saw him by the gate. He'd changed that much. They invited me to stay and have dinner with them, but I just drank some water, because I was in a hurry to get back to my own family. I wanted to get home to my family as fast as possible. I wanted to see if they were alive . . . and if they were still here, if they would be happy to see me. (*silence*)

A

What was his name?

D

Who?

A

The one you were talking about.

D

His name? What does it matter?

A

No. (*In silence, A walks over to the mattress where C is, and then carefully gets in under the blanket. She is on her back, looking into the dusk.*)

D

Aren't you going to lie down here?

A

I usually sleep here.

D

Come and lie here with me. (*silence*) Come here. (*pause*) Here. (*A slowly goes over to his mattress and crawls in next to him.*) Why are you dressed? (*silence*) Why are you wearing your clothes?

A

I . . .

D

Why?

A

I'm cold.

D

Cold? (*short pause*) Are you cold?

A

Yes.

D

I'll warm you up. (*He takes her hand. It has no wedding ring.*)

A

I had to sell it.

D

They took mine. (*silence*)

A

Good night. (*silence*)

D

Turn around.

A

Let's sleep.

                    D

Sleep?

                    A

Sleep.

                    D

Yes.

                    A

I'm tired.

                    D

No . . . you can sleep later. . . . Turn around.

                    A

No . . . I want to . . .

                    D

Do as I say. (*silence*)

                    A

No, don't.

                    D

Come on.

                    A

No, don't.

                    D

What's wrong with you?

                    A

I don't want to.

                    D

What don't you want?

A

No. (*silence*)

D

I want to be with you. . . . Don't you understand that?

A

I can't.

D

You can't?

A

No.

D

Why?

A

I can't.

D

Why? (*pause*) Is it because I'm blind?

A

No.

D

It still works, you know.

A

It's not because you're blind.

D

Is that why you don't want me?

A

Why can't we sleep?

D

To hell with sleep. I didn't come home to sleep. I want to have what I have the right to have.

A

Take your hands away.

D

I want what's mine.

A

It's not yours. Nothing is yours. Don't touch me.

D

I'll touch you as much as I want, wherever I want. What the hell is wrong with you? (*hits her*) Don't move, or I'll get really angry. Don't make me angry. Don't force me to give you a real beating. (*hits her*) Do as I say.

A

Sure. Go on, hit me. Just hit me.

D

(*hits her*) I don't want to beat you up. I've never hit you before.

A

Go on, hit me.

D

(*hits her*) Don't you hear me?

A

Do whatever you want.

D

I don't want to. I don't want to hit you.

A

You can rape me if you want to.

D

Rape you? How could I? A husband can't rape his own wife.

A

That's already happened . . . again and again.

D

What?

A

You or somebody else, it doesn't matter any longer.

D

No . . . no . . . (*silence*) Who? . . . Who?

A

It doesn't matter.

D

Who was it? Who did that to you?

A

It doesn't matter.

D

Who was it?

A

Everybody.

D

There were several? (*short pause*) Was there anyone I know?

A

Men . . . Ordinary men, like you. . . . Some were my students.

D

Have they stuck it in you? Did they stick their dirty cocks inside you?
(*silence*) Tell me who they were. . . . I'll kill them. I'll fucking kill them
all.

A

Yes, do that.

D

First I'll kill them and then I'll kill you. (*silence*) If you'd had any
decency in your body you should've taken your own life.

A

Yes.

D

Before I came home. . . . Then I would've avoided the shame. (*pause*)
You're made of shit. (*is flailing violently around himself*) The girls . . .
(*silence*) my girls? . . . (*silence*)

A

Why would they've been spared? (*silence*) The first ones who came were
Marco and his sons. . . . They just laughed.

D

Marco? (*pause*) Our neighbor? (*short pause*) Not Marco.

A

He just laughed.

D

Not him, not Marco.

A

He and his sons. . . . They were drunk. . . . They'd been drinking since
morning.

D

No. (*pause*) We're . . . but we know each other. We play the lottery together, and soccer. I used to help him with his car when it needed repair.

A

Him and his two sons.

D

They were always over here. . . . You used to have you hair done where
his wife works.

A

They forced me to look on while they were doing it. . . . Hour after hour
. . . after hour . . .

(*darkness*)

7.

(*light*)

(*D has walked outside. He can't scream. He sits still in the darkness,
stands up, and then sits down again.*)

D

Who is it? (*B coming back looks tired and pale. D stands up.*) I'll shoot.
. . . I have a gun. (*short pause*) Tell me who it is, otherwise I'll shoot.

B

Cut it out.

D

Beenina?

B

Yeah. . . . What are you doing?

D

Is that you?

B

What are you going to shoot with?

D

I didn't know who it was. . . . It could've been anyone.

B

You would have been dead by now.

D

What are you doing up so late?

B

Late? It's morning.

D

It is? What time is it?

B

I don't know.

D

Where are you going?

B

What about it?

D

Answer me properly.

B

I'm going to bed. I'm tired.

D

Have you been out? (*silence*) Wait.

B

What?

D

Stay here and talk to me. . . . Come over here.

B

What do you want?

D

I want to talk to you.

B

Why?

D

Why? I'm . . . (*short pause*) there's a lot that . . . you understand?
(*reaches out with his hand*) Come here.

B

I am here.

D

Closer . . . where are you?

B

What is it?

D

Yes, dear Beenina, give me your hand. (*again reaches for her with his
hand*) I'm . . .

B

What? Can't you see? (*B takes his hand unwillingly.*)

D

There. (*staggers slightly*) No, you know . . . You shouldn't be out running around during the night. . . . You never know what could happen.

B

Well, it's peaceful now.

D

Yes, but you never know what kind of crazies are running loose.

B

I'm OK.

D

Yes. . . . Don't be too sure.

B

There aren't any left. . . . The ones that are still here want to leave.

D

Where would they go?

B

Well . . . here there's nothing.

D

Soon everything will be like before.

B

As if that's any better.

D

Do you want to leave too? Go away?

B

What's there to do here?

D

Where?

B

Wherever. Some say they're going to America, but they're just dreaming.

D

Yes, I suppose it's nice there. . . . People think so, anyway. But it's probably the same there as it is here really . . . if you don't have money.

B

There's work in Italy. A lot of girls work there.

D

What kind of fucking jobs?

B

I don't know. . . . Maids . . . in hotels . . .

D

Yeah, jobs like that you can find here and there. . . . You don't have to go to Italy for that. (*pause*) Stay here with me.

B

I am.

D

Closer . . . where are you?

B

Here.

D

(*reaches out with his hand again*) Sit with me. (*pulls her closer, hugs her.*) You can sit in my lap . . . like when you were a little girl.

B

No . . . I'm too big.

D

You aren't too big to sit in my lap.

B

Yes, I am.

D

Don't you remember when I used to play with you? Don't you remember
how good I was to you? . . . I gave you a rabbit to play with . . . with big
ears. . . . Do you remember? Do you remember how it was trembling?
(*short pause*) What was his name? Do you remember?

B

I'm not a child.

D

No.

B

I'm not a child any more.

D

No . . . So, what are you?

B

I'm nothing.

D

So what are you? (*is holding her closer*) Are you a woman? (*silence*)
Have you become a woman?

B

There are no children any more.

D

Be quiet. (*caresses her hair*) What's happened to your hair?

B

I've cut it off.

D

It was so beautiful.

B

I had to . . . because nothing was happening . . .

D

You looked so good with your long, dark hair.

B

It was a change anyway.

D

Women are supposed to have long, long, beautiful hair. . . . Women aren't supposed to look like men and behave like men.

B

One day all women cut their hair off.

D

That's sick.

B

Easier to keep clean anyway.

D

So, go and paint your lips. (*silence*) How quiet it is.

B

(*tries to stand up*) I want to go now.

D

No, stay. (*silence*) Tell me.

B

What?

D

Tell me.

B

I've nothing to tell.

D

Do you have a boyfriend?

B

No.

D

No? (*pause*) You haven't been with a boy yet? (*silence*) Have you?

B

No.

D

Since you're a big girl now . . . since you have breasts and everything.

B

No.

D

I can feel it.

B

You're hurting me.

D

Stay here. Be kind.

B

Let go of me.

D

You're staying here with me . . .

B

Daddy.

D

Someone has to stay with me.

B

Daddy, stop it.

D

You have no daddy. You have nothing. Me neither.

B

You're gross. You're just like all the others.

(*B gets loose from his grip. Her blouse rips. On her back is a big scar in the shape of a cross that has been cut between her shoulder blades. E comes out. He has been in the bedroom with A. He looks at D. D has the feeling that there is someone there.*)

D

Sorry. (*silence*) It's not my fault. (*silence*) You have to listen to . . . (*silence*) Who is it? (*short pause*) Is it you? (*silence*) Answer me. (*short pause*) I know there's someone there. (*He stands up and starts to walk around. He is still wearing the long, dirty, dark-grey military coat that he has been wearing the whole time.*) So come here then. Come here and jerk me off. (*E wants to say something to him but can't.*) Answer me! (*short pause)* Who is it!

(*darkness*)

8.

(*light*)

(*Everyone is sitting outside the house. C is sitting between A and E. The light is very strong. C is drumming with her fingers on the chair and is humming a tune, which she often does. E puts his hand over her drumming hand.*)

A

(*to B*) Aren't you eating?

D

I don't want any more. (*pushes away the bread*)

A

OK, then. (*silence*)

D

Today will be a warm day. (*pause*) It's going to get warm today, I said.

A

Yes. (*to C, who has started with the drumming again*) Stop it.

D

Yes, stop doing that, or I'll break your fingers off. (*silence, turns towards A*) So, what are you doing today?

A

Who?

D

You. I'm talking to you. (*silence*)

A

I'm going into the village.

D

What are you doing in the village?

A

I'll be waiting.

D

Waiting?

A

I'll be waiting to see if there's a food package.

C

There hasn't been one for a whole week.

A

You have to go there anyway. (*silence*)

C

When I'm big I'll strap bombs all around my body and go into the church and blow them up in so many pieces that there is nothing left of them. Poof.

(*A stands up and puts her hand over C's mouth.*)

D

Did you start cooking the potatoes?

A

And where would I get them?

D

Are we supposed to starve then?

(*C is drumming.*)

A

(*hits C*) Stop it!

C

Stop it yourself. (*E takes her hand and holds it.*) There were people here from German and English TV who talked to Mommy and Beenina after the soldiers were here and took all the men. Beenina didn't know many words then. Now she knows a lot of bad words.

D

Yes, back then there were as many journalists in this country as flies on a corpse.

C
Now there's no one who wants to ask us anything.

E
(*quietly*) I'm leaving now.

A
(*quietly*) Wait for me.

D
What did you say?

A
Nothing.

C
There was an old lady who gave me a pair of sunglasses, but Mommy sold them. (*silence*)

E
(*quietly*) Let's go.

C
I want to come too.

A
No, you stay here.

C
Why?

A
Because I said so.

C
Uncle Ivan, why can't I go too?

D

Ivan?

A

Yes, she was thinking about him.

C

Yeah, I said the wrong thing.

D

Why did you say "Ivan?"

A

Yes, she's been talking a lot about him. She was so sad when he disappeared.

C

Yes, I was thinking about him. I was thinking about Uncle Ivan. He's a martyr. He's a real martyr. An old martyr with old, ugly glasses.

D

He doesn't become a martyr just because he's dead.

C

No. (*silence*)

D

Where's Beenina?

A

She's here.

D

Aha. . . . Is there a pick around?

A

A pick? For what?

D

I'm going to loosen up the goddamn earth so that we'll be able to plant something.

A

What are you going to plant?

D

I'll put in any kind of shit. As long as it grows. There must be something. The girls can go out and look for seeds and bulbs. They can look in the houses and the yards where nobody lives any more. If they find any flower bulbs we could plant them and sell the flowers. Otherwise they'll have to go out there and beg.

A

There isn't anyone who has anything.

D

No, not here, but out there, on the big highway.

A

Wouldn't it be better if you went? You are blind. It's easier for people to give to someone who's blind.

D

I've never begged. I'm not a beggar.

A

They aren't either.

D

No, but they'll forget. I won't.

A

They'll never forget. (*silence*)

C

Mommy, can I have her bread?

A

No.

C

She doesn't want it.

A

No, I said.

C

Why?

A

No.

C

Fucking cunt. You're crazy.

(*A hits her.*)

D

(*grabs C's arm and hits her*) If you say that word one more time I'll whip you to death.

C

Like I give a shit.

A

She doesn't know what she's saying.

C

Of course I do. (*E stands up.*) Maybe I'll say something.

D

What?

A

You'd better not say anything.

C

If I can't go with you . . .

(*A walks into the house.*)

D

Did she leave? (*D gives his bread to C.*)

C

I don't want it.

(*darkness*)

9.

(*light*)

(*E sits down across from D. D feels uncomfortable but doesn't know why. E wants to tell D that he exists, but he can't. He reaches out his hand to touch D, but he can't. A comes out.*)

D

Is that you?

A

Yes. (*She tells E quietly to leave, but E doesn't move. B leaves.*)

D

Are you on your way?

A

Soon.

D

To the village? (*silence*) You're going to the village, right? (*silence*) When are you coming back?

A

Later, I guess. (*silence*)

D

You'll be back, won't you?

A

What else can I do?

D

Yes, since you have the kids to take care of. (*E stands up. D is about to leave and touches E.*) Wait.

A

I have to go now.

D

What am I supposed to do?

A

(*quietly*) What can you do? . . . It is what it is.

D

I can't even get even. There's no one to get even with. There's nothing I can do. . . . How do you think that feels? How do you think it feels to live in darkness? I tell myself I'll get used to it after a while, but I know that will never happen. A dog is worth more. . . . At least the dog doesn't know and might find someone to take care of it, help it, so that it doesn't suffer needlessly when there's no hope. (*He falls silent and is sitting still, then turns around as if he feels the presence of someone else.*)

(*darkness*)

10.

(*light*)

(*C comes out. D turns to her.*)

C

It's just me. . . . (*playacting war*) Look up, look up! All children, go and find shelter! Go and hide! . . . Mommy, my arm, my arm. . . . Daddy, Daddy (*goes up to him*), I don't know what to do.

D

Is there someone else here?

C

You're here.

D

It's getting too warm sitting here. Help me to find some shade. (*C takes his hand and leads him into the shade*.) Where are we going?

C

We're going to Italy.

D

(*sits down*) Yes, it's better here. . . . Where are the others?

C

Mommy's in town.

D

And your sister?

C

I haven't seen her. She's always gone. I'm always home by myself, but it doesn't matter. I like it. Then I can think much better. When I'm big I'll always be alone. Then I can do whatever I want. I can go out and come back whenever I want. Then no one can tell me what to wear. If I don't want to eat, or if I just want to stay in bed, I can do it. I think I'll write books. They'll be published in many languages, so that I can travel to all those countries where my books are, but no one will know who I am. I am free. I'll smoke lots of cigarettes and stay up all night and listen to music. I won't eat any food, because it's easier to write books when you're hungry. I won't get married. I don't believe in love, but I'll buy a

house for Mommy and Daddy when I get a lot of money. (*silence*)
Maybe I can even pay a doctor to do an operation on you so you can see
again.

D

I don't want to see again. (*silence*)

C

Daddy.

D

There's only shit to see. Be quiet now.

C

What if . . .

D

What?

C

What if he isn't dead?

D

Who's not dead?

C

What if Uncle Ivan is alive? What if he isn't dead?

D

Why wouldn't he be?

C

Would that make you happy?

D

Why would I be happy? (*short pause*) I don't know if I can be happy any
more.

C

Why? Because of the war?

D

I've never been happy. I've worked. I've never had time to be happy or anything else.

C

But if he came here . . . what would you do?

D

Well, what would I do?

C

Would he be allowed to live here with us?

D

Yes . . . but he'd have to do his part. (*short pause*) But he won't.

C

What?

D

Come back.

C

Why?

D

Because no one comes back. . . . We're created by God and one day we'll return to him . . . and stay there.

C

I know. (*silence*) Daddy.

D

I'm going to take a nap.

C

I know something.

D

Yeah . . . yeah.

C

That I'm not allowed to say. (*silence*) I followed after Beenina to the station even though I wasn't allowed. There this old guy came up to her and talked to her. He was fat. I think he works there, at the station. Then they left and I followed them. They went into this house, and I just wanted to know why she went there, so I followed her. They went in to see someone who lived there. Then she saw me and got angry and told me to go home. But then this old woman who lived there came out and told me to stay. And then they argued with each other and she said I could do whatever I wanted; and she took me out on a balcony and asked me how old I was. I said I was eleven, because that's what I was then. Then the old guy came out and said that I was much too young, but she said I should do what he said, if I wanted to; but he said that I was just a goddamn kid; but then she said that I could come there whenever I wanted, and then she said that I should go with him to this little room where there was just a mattress on the floor; and then he came in, and then he did it with me, even though he had said that he didn't want to.

(*darkness*)

11.

(*light*)

(*E is sitting outside. A is straightening up. B and C are sitting in a corner.*)

E

No. (*silence*) I can't.

A

No, then you can't.

E

Don't you understand that?

A

Yeah . . .

E

I'm not made that way. (*silence*) He's my brother . . . I can't do it.

A

Who could then?

E

No.

A

There were many things one thought one couldn't do.

E

Yes.

A

Before the war. . . . That was a different time. (*E pulls his shirt over his head and makes a sound of pain.*) Does it hurt?

E

It'll always hurt. (*pause*) I think we should just leave instead.

A

Where? Where would we go?

E

What the hell, wherever . . . where we don't have to remember. We could get out of here today. We could try to find someplace where we could start over . . . where no one knows us, where we'd start clean.

A

How, without money and food?

E

It couldn't be worse than here. Let's go.

A

I don't have the strength to go anywhere.

E

I don't know what to do. . . . I can't stay here. Sometimes it feels as if he was looking at me, as if he sees me, as if he knew I was here. . . . It's as if he's just playing with me. He always hated me. He resented me when I was young because I was into books and had my own thoughts, instead of being into soccer and cars, and had no interest in business. As often as he could he'd slap me or kick me and tell me to go out and go to work.

A

And now you've taken his wife.

E

Why do you say that?

A

Since I belong to him.

E

I haven't taken anything you haven't given to me. It happened when I thought you were all alone. You weren't his any longer.

A

Now I am.

E

No.

A

As long as he's alive, I am.

E

No, you're mine.

A

Am I?

E

Yes, you're mine. (*holds her*)

A

What are you going to do with me?

E

Listen to you. We've got to leave. Pack up some of the things you'll need and then we'll leave tonight, while the others are asleep.

A

The others?

E

Yes.

A

What others?

E

The others.

A

Do you mean the children? (*short pause*) Aren't they coming?

E

That's not possible.

A

Do you mean for me to leave them here?

E

We can't take them with us. Then we won't get anywhere; we'll send for them once we're settled.

A

Do you really think I'd leave them?

E

It's just temporary . . . until we find something.

A

No.

E

They have their father.

A

I won't go anywhere without them.

E

Someone has to stay and take care of him.

A

I won't leave without them. You'll have to go by yourself.

B and C

(*together*) Sssshh.

(*D comes out, falls over something, then stands up.*)

E

I am going to tell him.

D

(*looks around*) Is there someone here? (*silence*) Who is it?

A

What do you want?

D

Who are you talking to? Who is that?

                    A

Who?

                    D

The one you're talking to?

                    A

There's no one here.

                    D

I thought I heard someone . . . I thought I heard voices . . . I thought I was still in the camp and was going over to the latrine. . . . The one who was sleeping in the same cot as I had died during the night. . . . He was some kind of engineer. He was very good at keeping clean. . . . He had gotten hold of a little piece of soap that he kept between his butt cheeks, because you weren't allowed to have those things. I thought I heard you talking to someone.

                    A

It's just me.

                    D

Just You? (*short pause*) I thought I heard voices.

                    A

Go back to bed.

                    D

What did you say?

                    A

I can't stand looking at you. Go away.

                    D

What are you saying, you goddamn bitch? Is that how you talk to a war hero who has given his eyes for his country?

A

War hero? You?

D

Yes, I am. Show some respect.

A

You fucking idiot, what kind of hero comes home like a beggar and lets his own daughter sell her body every night?

D

That's enough. I've had it. I've had enough of this shit. I'll show who's the boss! (*walks around, gets more and more desperate, swings at her, throws things in the air, falls down, stands up*) What the hell, stay still. Stay still so I can kill you. (*E starts to laugh. A laughs too.*) Who's that? (*pause*) Who's laughing?

(*darkness*)

12.

(*light*)

(*B comes back. E is sitting. B sits down on a chair, lights a cigarette, and pulls off her shoes.*)

E

Do you have a cigarette? (*B gives him the pack.*) American?

B

Yes. (*silence*)

E

How are things? (*silence*) Good?

B

I have such fucking pains in my feet.

E

Your feet?

B

These fucking shoes. . . . I don't have the strength to walk any more. (*silence*)

E

(*gives her a cup of tea*) Want some? (*B doesn't answer and shrugs.*) It's gotten cold. (*silence*) So, how was the night?

B

(*shrugs again*) Same as usual. (*silence*) Fucking fog. Couldn't see anything. Couldn't see the cars until they'd almost passed. There was this big motherfucking truck that almost killed me.

E

Yes, it's humid tonight.

B

But then he stopped. I didn't know if I should go over to him, but I did. I had to walk the whole fucking way. (*short pause*) Then he wanted to find a place to park before we did anything. So we had to walk for miles. And there wasn't any water there, so you couldn't wash up.

E

Where?

B

In the toilets there, at the rest stop.

E

OK.

B

There are some fucking horrible places out there.

E

Once it was so beautiful. (*pause*) I guess there are more cars on the road
these days.

B

Seems like it.

E

But you're young.

B

Not so young any more.

E

They want them as young as possible I guess.

B

Most of them are younger than me. I'm old compared to them.

E

I guess they have the most money.

B

Who?

E

Those who want the youngest ones.

B

No, there are all kinds. . . . The Russians are the worst. They just push
you out of the car and take off when they've gotten what they want. They
are fucking pigs. (*silence*) Are you taking off?

E

Where to?

B

Away from here.

E

Why do you think that?

B

Are you? (*short pause*) Answer me.

E

 I don't know. . . . I should.

B

Yes, me too. (*silence*) Where to?

E

Where to?

B

Yes.

E

Somewhere. . . . Wherever.

B

Yes. (*silence*) Why can't I come?

E

You? (*short pause*) With me?

B

Yes. (*silence*) Can I? Can I come with you?

E

But I don't know where I'm going.

B

It's better if you're two.

E

It won't work. . . . What would your mother say?

B

Her? She doesn't give a damn what I do. She's never cared about me. Because then she wouldn't have let me . . . no mother would've let me do what I do. A real mother would've rather killed herself.

E

It's not easy for her.

B

For her?

E

It can't be easy . . . knowing . . .

B

Easier than for me anyway.

E

I guess she's doing the best she can.

B

Sure. (*silence*) I'll do anything . . . just to get away from here.

E

What? What is it that you would do?

B

I'll be nice, do anything you want me to do. As long as you take me with you.

E

Do you think it's better some other place?

B

Anything is better than here. (*pause*) Tomorrow I'm going to throw myself in front of a car . . . if I can't come with you. I don't feel like living anyway. I might as well be dead. Like all the others—Biljana, Hakile, Fezlic, Advija . . .

(*darkness*)

13.

(*light*)

(*D is sitting on a chair. C is sitting on the ground playing. A comes out. The sunshine is strong.*)

A
Where's she? (*silence*) Where's that goddamn whore? Where's she?

C
Mommy, you're scaring me.

A
(*goes over to C*) Where did she go?

C
I don't know. She was here yesterday.

A
You know where she is. You always know where she is.

C
No.

A
Tell me! (*grabs C, shakes her*) Tell me where she went.

C
Mommy, I don't know. It's true.

A
Don't lie. (*hits her*)

C
It's true. I'm not lying.

A
You know where she is. You know everything.

C
No.

A
You keep track of everyone.

C
No, I don't know anything.

A
Now you tell me where she is or I'll kill you!

D
What's the goddamn screaming for? (*stands up*)

C
Mommy, I don't know. It's true.

A
(*hits C*) Tell me!

C
I'm just a child.

D
What the hell are you doing?

A
Did she go with him? Did he take her with him?

D
What the hell are you fighting about?

C
When I woke up she wasn't there. . . . She was gone.

D

Could you keep your mouths shut? Think about what I've been through. I need some peace and quiet. I didn't come home to have to listen to screaming women. I need to rest. I need to get my strength back.

A

Just leave us alone, you fucking cripple.

D

What did you say?

A

You don't understand anything. You were blind even before you became blind. (*walks into the house*)

D

What the hell is this? Where am I? Who do you think I am? Soon you'll be telling me how to wipe my ass. Hell, I've had enough of this. You'd better start behaving like a decent person. I've been through a war. I've been out there defending my country and my family, my father and my mother, my wife and my children. I've looked death in the eye every morning and every night. I've been alone with death. I could've done what Ivan did, put a little vial of blood in my mouth and bit into it, while they were examining me, so that they thought I was too sick to go to war. Him, you can say nice things about all day, this ass who ran away and hid. I've experienced things no human being should. Maybe I'm blind, but I'm still a human being. It's my right to be respected. I want you to treat me with respect, otherwise you'll see what I'll do to you. Do you hear me? Do you hear what I'm saying? (*pause*) Do you hear what I'm saying? (*silence*)

C

She isn't here . . . She went inside. I'm the only one here. (*silence*)

D

I'm not asking for anything more than I have the right to. . . . Basic human . . .

C

Beenina ran away.

D

Beenina?

C

She took all her clothes.

D

Well . . . what about it?

C

Maybe she'll never come back again.

D

I can't do anything about that.

C

She said she would do it one of these days.

D

One of these days.

(*A comes out*)

C

Mommy . . . what are you going to do?

A

Come here.

C

What are you going to do?

A

I'm going to get her.

C

I want to go too.

A

No. You stay here.

C

No.

A

Stay here until I'm back. You stay and look after him.

C

No . . . Mommy.

A

Do what I tell you . . . I'll be back.

C

No.

A

I'll be back later. You're a big girl now.

C

I don't want to . . . I don't want to be alone.

A

You're a big girl now. You'll be all right. I'll be back later.

C

I'm not a big girl. (*A leaves.*)

(*darkness*)

14.

(*light*)

D

(*sitting on the mattress with C lying next to him*) I was lying in the same cot. . . . I was sharing a cot with a doctor. . . . We didn't speak the same language, we didn't understand what we said to each other . . . still we understood each other somehow . . . still we could talk to each other about one thing or another . . . about our homes . . . our work . . . our families . . . what our children looked like . . . what they did . . . what they used to play with. . . . The cot was so narrow that we had to turn at the same time. . . . Finally we knew each other so well that when the other wanted to turn to the other side we did it together, in our sleep. . . . He had two sons. . . . I told him I had two daughters . . . and that they were always happy, always singing. He told me his boy was taking piano lessons. He'd lost his right leg.

C

In the war?

D

Not the boy. The dad. He'd lost his right leg. When he came to the camp they took away his artificial leg. He had to jump around on one leg when he was going to work. He was very fat. He weighed at least two hundred and fifty pounds. He came from the far north. His name was Zadek. He died later. But they didn't like that we were talking to each other, so they kept playing American pop music all night.

C

What kind of music?

D

Don't know. It was the same shit over and over again. (*pause*) After a few months we were moved to a factory where they made tractors. They knew I was a skilled mechanic, so I had it a little easier there. One night after "lights out" a couple of officers came with their girlfriends. They were wearing beautiful uniforms and evening gowns as if they were going to a party. But they were already drunk and looking for some fun, so they came down to stare at the monkeys. One of them was going to show off in front of the others. He ordered one of my buddies to hold a cigarette lighter against my eyes. His face was the last thing I saw . . . my buddy . . . (*silence*) One of these days I'll find him, that officer. One day my turn will come. One day I'll get revenge. (*lies down*)

C

Just think if mommy never comes back.

D

Yes, now go to sleep.

C

Yes.

D

Now go to sleep and she'll be back.

C

Mommy is dead. But we'll still manage. I can go begging tomorrow if you come with me.

D

Yes, I'll stand a little behind you and make sure that nothing happens. (*silence*) Now go to sleep.

(*E comes into the house and walks up to the mattress. C is looking at E and sits up.*)

E

Be quiet.

C

Where's mommy?

(*E makes a sign to be silent and to follow him. C tries to quietly get up from the mattress as she looks at E. C notices the book behind the pillow and is about to reach for it. D wakes up and holds her in a hard grip. C makes a sound of being in pain.*)

D

Oh, it's you . . . I thought it was her.

C

It's just me.

D

Sleep now. (*pause*) Now go back to sleep. (*E makes a sign for her to come. C nods and tries to get away from D's arms.*) Now let's sleep and dream about how it once was . . . before the war.

C

I have to pee.

D

OK.

C

(*She points to her book and whispers.*) My book.

E

(*He shakes his head and whispers.*) Forget it.

(*C uses mime to show that she must have it. E tiptoes as quietly as he can over to the bed and bends over D to grab the book. D, who senses another presence, grabs E's hand. D gets so frightened that he swings at the air and hits E in the face. E tries to get loose. D grabs E's face and feels it all over.*)

D

(*after a moment of silence, quietly*) Ivan? (*silence*) Ivan? Is that you?

E

Yes, it's me.

D

Is it you? What are you doing here? How are you?

E

I heard you were home.

D

Yes.

E

I thought that . . . I thought I should come and see you.

(*They stand up.*)

D

Never thought this would happen.

E

No.

D

That we would see each other again.

E

No, that . . .

D

You probably thought I was dead.

E

Yeah, one didn't really know . . . (*silence*)

D

What do you want?

E

What do I want? (*short pause*) Well . . .

D

Why do you come here in the middle of the night?

E

Well . . . I don't know. (*silence*)

D

What did you say?

E

Nothing . . . I didn't say anything. (*C is standing still in the middle of the room. She has decided that she is not going out.*) You're my brother . . .

D

So what?

E

You are, aren't you . . . even if I'm not the brother you'd wanted? (*laughs*) I guess it is what it is. You can think whatever you want. We've never been able to talk to each other . . . about anything important.

D

I guess we haven't had that much to say to each other. One can live without it.

E

Yes.

D

Well . . . well. (*silence*)

E

I came here to say . . . I thought I would say goodbye.

D

Really . . . you're going away?

E

Yes, there's nothing for me to do here. Only ruins are left. . . . People are just hanging around, hoping someone will take care of them . . . but no one will. . . . I don't know what to say. . . . We've been living in darkness for so long that we can't see the light. . . . But the bodies that were left in the streets are gone. . . . They are gone now. . . . People you knew . . . people you went to school with . . . they were left there for weeks. . . . Not even the dogs cared about them. . . . You mustn't think that it has been easy here either. (*laughs*) To live here . . . if that's what you were thinking . . . one didn't know at what moment death would come. . . . One didn't know if one was dead or alive. . . . That's when you do things you never thought you were capable of. . . . It's as if someone else was doing it. . . . You don't understand, do you?

D

What are you talking about?

E

Nothing. How it was.

D

One shouldn't think about those things. . . . Now we have to look forward. . . . That other stuff we might as well forget.

E

I even had to kill your white dog so we'd have something to eat. (*silence*)

D

I guess the soccer games will start up again soon. (*pause*) Is it dark?

E

Dark?

D

Outside.

E

No, it's light.

D

Isn't it night?

E

No . . . it's morning.

D

It feels like . . . like it was night. (*pause*) How's Omer?

E

Omer?

D

Yes, your son . . . (*silence*) You did have a son, right?

E

Yes, I did have a son.

D

He must be a big boy now . . . ten, eleven years old . . .

E

No.

D

How old is he now?

E

He's dead.

D

Aha.

E

He died.

D

Yes. (*silence*)

E

They made me whip him . . . whip him . . . whip him until he died. (*He makes a motion to C to leave.*)

C

(*shakes her head*) No.

(*darkness*)

THE END

Major Plays by Lars Norén

1979	ORESTES
1981	A TERRIBLE HAPPINESS
1981	MUNICH – ATHENS
1981	SMILES OF THE INFERNO
1982	NIGHT IS MOTHER TO THE DAY
1982	CHAOS IS THE NEIGHBOR OF GOD
1982	DEMONS
1983	THE LAST SUPPER
1984	CLAUDIO (MANTEGNA PORTOFOLIO)
1985	THE COMEDIANS
1986	FLOWERS OF OUR TIME
1987	HEBRIANA
1988	AUTUMN AND WINTER
1988	BOBBY FISCHER LIVES IN PASADENA
1988	AND GIVE US THE SHADOWS
1989	TRUTH OR DARE
1989	SUMMER
1990	LOVE MADE SIMPLE
1990	CHINNON
1991	THE LAST QUARTET
1991	LOST AND FOUND
1991	THE LEAVES IN VALLOMBROSA
1992	MOIRE DI –
1992	STERBLICH
1994	ROMANIANS
1994	BLOOD
1994	A KIND OF HADES
1994	THE CLINIC
1994	TRIO TO THE END OF THE WORLD
1997	PERSONKRETS 3:1
1998	SEVEN/THREE
1998	SHADOW BOYS
2000	NOVEMBER
2000	ACT
2000	COMING AND GOING
2002	QUIET WATERS

2003   DETAILS
2003   CHILL
2005   WAR
2006   TERMINAL
2007   ANNA POLITKOVSKIA
2010   ORESTIEN
2012   FRAGMENTE
2013   3.31.93

Acknowledgments

A big thank you to David van Asselt for having produced *War* at the Rattlestick Playwright's Theater in New York in 2006, and for writing the foreword to this book of translations.

I want to thank Ulrika Josephsson for being our "fairy godmother" for the production of *War*, and for sharing her deep insights and knowledge of the play with me and the cast.

As always I want to thank my dear husband, Len Gochman, for his never-ending support.

Again, with gratitude, I thank Jane and Richard Altschuler for their guidance and patience, and their strong belief bringing Norén plays to an American audience.

www.ingramcontent.com/pod-product-compliance
Ingram Content Group UK Ltd.
Pitfield, Milton Keynes, MK11 3LW, UK
UKHW040113171224
3689UKWH00031B/227

9 781884 092893